Grisly Grisell

THE LAIDLY LADY OF WHITBURN

A TALE OF THE WARSOF THE ROSES

Charlotte M. Yonge

1st WORLD
LIBRARY
Literary Society

Grisly Grisell

Charlotte M. Yonge

© 1st World Library – Literary Society, 2005
PO Box 2211
Fairfield, IA 52556
www.1stworldlibrary.org
First Edition

LCCN: 2004195602

Softcover ISBN: 1-4218-0423-9
Hardcover ISBN: 1-4218-0323-2
eBook ISBN: 1-4218-0523-5

Purchase *"Grisly Grisell"*
as a traditional bound book at:
www.1stWorldLibrary.org/purchase.asp?ISBN=1-4218-0423-9

1st World Library Literary Society is a nonprofit
organization dedicated to promoting literacy by:

- Creating a free internet library accessible from any computer worldwide.
- Hosting writing competitions and offering book publishing scholarships.

Grisly Grisell
contributed by Tim, Ed & Rodney
in support of
1st World Library Literary Society

CHAPTER I

AN EXPLOSION

It was a great pity, so it was, this villanous saltpetre should be digg'd out of the bowels of the harmless earth.

SHAKESPEARE King Henry IV., Part I.

A terrible shriek rang through the great Manor-house of Amesbury. It was preceded by a loud explosion, and there was agony as well as terror in the cry. Then followed more shrieks and screams, some of pain, some of fright, others of anger and recrimination. Every one in the house ran together to the spot whence the cries proceeded, namely, the lower court, where the armourer and blacksmith had their workshops.

There was a group of children, the young people who were confided to the great Earl Richard and Countess Alice of Salisbury for education and training. Boys and girls were alike there, some of the latter crying and sobbing, others mingling with the lads in the hot dispute as to "who did it."

By the time the gentle but stately Countess had reached the place, all the grown-up persons of the establishment - knights, squires, grooms, scullions, and females of every degree - had thronged round them, but parted at her approach, though one of the knights said, "Nay, Lady Countess, 'tis no sight for you. The poor little maid is dead, or nigh upon it."

"But who is it? What is it?" asked the Countess, still advancing.

A confused medley of voices replied, "The Lord of Whitburn's little wench - Leonard Copeland - gunpowder."

"And no marvel," said a sturdy, begrimed figure, "if the malapert young gentles be let to run all over the courts, and handle that with which they have no concern, lads and wenches alike."

"Nay, how can I stop it when my lady will not have the maidens kept ever at their distaffs and needles in seemly fashion," cried a small but stout and self-assertive dame, known as "Mother of the Maidens," then starting, "Oh! my lady, I crave your pardon, I knew not you were in this coil! And if the men-at-arms be let to have their perilous goods strewn all over the place, no wonder at any mishap."

"Do not wrangle about the cause," said the Countess. "Who is hurt? How much?"

The crowd parted enough for her to make way to where a girl of about ten was lying prostrate and bleeding with her head on a woman's lap.

"Poor maid," was the cry, "poor maid! 'Tis all over with her. It will go ill with young Leonard Copeland."

"Worse with Hodge Smith for letting him touch his irons."

"Nay, what call had Dick Jenner to lay his foul, burning gunpowder - a device of Satan - in this yard? A mercy we are not all blown to the winds."

The Countess, again ordering peace, reached the girl, whose moans showed that she was still alive, and between the barber-surgeon and the porter's wife she was lifted up, and carried to a bed, the Countess Alice keeping close to her, though the "Mother of the Maidens," who was a somewhat helpless personage, hung back, declaring that the sight of the wounds made her swoon. There were terrible wounds upon the face and neck, which seemed to be almost bared of skin. The lady, who had been bred to some knowledge of surgical skill, together with the barber-surgeon, did their best to allay the agony with applications of sweet oil. Perhaps if they had had more of what was then considered skill, it might have been worse for her.

The Countess remained anxiously trying all that could allay the suffering of the poor little semi-conscious patient, who kept moaning for "nurse." She was Grisell Dacre, the daughter of the Baron of Whitburn, and had been placed, young as she was, in the household of the Countess of Salisbury on her mother being made one of the ladies attending on the young Queen Margaret of Anjou, lately married to King Henry VI.

Attendance on the patient had prevented the Countess from hearing the history of the accident, but presently the clatter of horses' feet showed that her lord was returning, and, committing the girl to her old nurse, she went down to the hall to receive him.

The grave, grizzled warrior had taken his seat on his cross-legged, round-backed chair, and a boy of some twelve years old stood before him, in a sullen attitude, one foot over the other, and his shoulder held fast by a squire, while the motley crowd of retainers stood behind.

There was a move at the entrance of the lady, and her husband rose, came forward, and as he gave her the courteous kiss of greeting, demanded, "What is all this coil? Is the little wench dead?"

"Nay, but I fear me she cannot live," was the answer.

"Will Dacre of Whitburn's maid? That's ill, poor child! How fell it out?"

"That I know as little as you," was the answer. "I have been seeing to the poor little maid's hurts."

Lord Salisbury placed her in the chair like his own. In point of fact, she was Countess in her own right; he, Richard Nevil, had been created Earl of Salisbury in her right on the death of her father, the staunch warrior of Henry V. in the siege of Orleans.

"Speak out, Leonard Copeland," said the Earl. "What hast thou done?"

The boy only growled, "I never meant to hurt the maid."

"Speak to the point, sir," said Lord Salisbury sternly; "give yourself at least the grace of truth."

Leonard grew more silent under the show of

Charlotte M. Yonge

displeasure, and only hung his head at the repeated calls to him to speak. The Earl turned to those who were only too eager to accuse him.

"He took a bar of iron from the forge, so please you, my lord, and put it to the barrel of powder."

"Is this true, Leonard?" demanded the Earl again, amazed at the frantic proceeding, and Leonard muttered "Aye," vouchsafing no more, and looking black as thunder at a fair, handsome boy who pressed to his side and said, "Uncle," doffing his cap, "so please you, my lord, the barrels had just been brought in upon Hob Carter's wain, and Leonard said they ought to have the Lord Earl's arms on them. So he took a bar of hot iron from the forge to mark the saltire on them, and thereupon there was this burst of smoke and flame, and the maid, who was leaning over, prying into his doings, had the brunt thereof."

"Thanks to the saints that no further harm was done," ejaculated the lady shuddering, while her lord proceeded - "It was not malice, but malapert meddling, then. Master Leonard Copeland, thou must be scourged to make thee keep thine hands off where they be not needed. For the rest, thou must await what my Lord of Whitburn may require. Take him away, John Ellerby, chastise him, and keep him in ward till we see the issue."

Leonard, with his head on high, marched out of the hall, not uttering a word, but shaking his shoulder as if to get rid of the squire's grasp, but only thereby causing himself to be gripped the faster.

Next, Lord Salisbury's severity fell upon Hob the

carter and Hodge the smith, for leaving such perilous wares unwatched in the court-yard. Servants were not dismissed for carelessness in those days, but soundly flogged, a punishment considered suitable to the "blackguard" at any age, even under the mildest rule. The gunner, being somewhat higher in position, and not in charge at the moment, was not called to account, but the next question was, how the "Mother of the Maids" - the gouvernante in charge of the numerous damsels who formed the train of the Lady of Salisbury, and were under education and training - could have permitted her maidens to stray into the regions appropriated to the yeomen and archers, and others of the meine, where they certainly had no business.

It appeared that the good and portly lady had last seen the girls in the gardens "a playing at the ball" with some of the pages, and that there, on a sunny garden seat, slumber had prevented her from discovering the absence of the younger part of the bevy. The demure elder damsels deposed that, at the sound of wains coming into the court, the boys had rushed off, and the younger girls had followed them, whether with or without warning was not made clear. Poor little Grisell's condition might have been considered a sufficient warning, nevertheless the two companions in her misdemeanour were condemned to a whipping, to enforce on them a lesson of maidenliness; and though the Mother of the Maids could not partake of the flagellation, she remained under her lord's and lady's grave displeasure, and probably would have to submit to a severe penance from the priest for her careless-ness. Yet, as she observed, Mistress Grisell was a North Country maid, never couthly or conformable, but like a boy, who would moreover always be after Leonard Copeland, whether he would or no.

Charlotte M. Yonge

It was the more unfortunate, as Lord Salisbury lamented to his wife, because the Copelands were devoted to the Somerset faction; and the King had been labouring to reconcile them to the Dacres, and to bring about a contract of marriage between these two unfortunate children, but he feared that whatever he could do, there would only be additional feud and bitterness, though it was clear that the mishap was accidental. The Lord of Whitburn himself was in Ireland with the Duke of York, while his lady was in attendance on the young Queen, and it was judged right and seemly to despatch to her a courier with the tidings of her daughter's disaster, although in point of fact, where a house could number sons, damsels were not thought of great value, except as the means of being allied with other houses. A message was also sent to Sir William Copeland that his son had been the death of the daughter of Whitburn; for poor little Grisell lay moaning in a state of much fever and great suffering, so that the Lady Salisbury could not look at her, nor hear her sighs and sobs without tears, and the barber-surgeon, unaccustomed to the effects of gunpowder, had little or no hope of her life.

Leonard Copeland's mood was sullen, not to say surly. He submitted to the chastisement without a word or cry, for blows were the lot of boys of all ranks, and were dealt out without much respect to justice; and he also had to endure a sort of captivity, in a dismal little circular room in a turret of the manorial house, with merely a narrow loophole to look out from, and this was only accessible by climbing up a steep broken slope of brick-work in the thickness of the wall.

Here, however, he was visited by his chief friend and comrade, Edmund Plantagenet of York, who found him lying on the floor, building up fragments of stone and mortar into the plan of a castle.

"How dost thou, Leonard?" he asked. "Did old Hal strike very hard?"

"I reck not," growled Leonard.

"How long will my uncle keep thee here?" asked Edmund sympathisingly.

"Till my father comes, unless the foolish wench should go and die. She brought it on me, the peevish girl. She is always after me when I want her least."

"Yea, is not she contracted to thee?"

"So they say; but at least this puts a stop to my being plagued with her - do what they may to me. There's an end to it, if I hang for it."

"They would never hang thee."

"None knows what you traitor folk of Nevil would do to a loyal house," growled Leonard.

"Traitor, saidst thou," cried Edmund, clenching his fists. "'Tis thy base Somerset crew that be the traitors."

"I'll brook no such word from thee," burst forth Leonard, flying at him.

"Ha! ha!" laughed Edmund even as they grappled. "Who is the traitor forsooth? Why, 'tis my father who should be King. 'Tis white-faced Harry and his Beauforts -"

The words were cut short by a blow from Leonard, and the warder presently found the two boys rolling on the floor together in hot contest.

And meanwhile poor Grisell was trying to frame with her torn and flayed cheeks and lips, "O lady, lady, visit it not on him! Let not Leonard be punished. It was my fault for getting into his way when I should have been in the garden. Dear Madge, canst thou speak for him?"

Madge was Edmund's sister, Margaret of York, who stood trembling and crying by Grisell's bed.

CHAPTER II

THE BROKEN MATCH

The Earl of Salisbury, called Prudence.

Contemporary Poem.

Little Grisell Dacre did not die, though day after day she lay in a suffering condition, tenderly watched over by the Countess Alice. Her mother had been summoned from attendance on the Queen, but at first there only was returned a message that if the maid was dead she should be embalmed and sent north to be buried in the family vault, when her father would be at all charges. Moreover, that the boy should be called to account for his crime, his father being, as the Lady of Whitburn caused to be written, an evil-minded minion and fosterer of the house of Somerset, the very bane of the King and the enemies of the noble Duke of York and Earl of Warwick.

The story will be clearer if it is understood that the Earl of Salisbury was Richard Nevil, one of the large family of Nevil of Raby Castle in Westmoreland, and had obtained his title by marriage with Alice Montagu, heiress of that earldom. His youngest sister had married Richard Plantagenet, Duke of York, who being descended from Lionel, Duke of Clarence, was

Charlotte M. Yonge

considered to have a better right to the throne than the house of Lancaster, though this had never been put forward since the earlier years of Henry V.

Salisbury had several sons. The eldest had married Anne Beauchamp, and was in her right Earl of Warwick, and had estates larger even than those of his father. He had not, however, as yet come forward, and the disputes at Court were running high between the friends of the Duke of Somerset and those of the Duke of York.

The King and Queen both were known to prefer the house of Somerset, who were the more nearly related to Henry, and the more inclined to uphold royalty, while York was considered as the champion of the people. The gentle King and the Beauforts wished for peace with France; the nation, and with them York, thought this was giving up honour, land, and plunder, and suspected the Queen, as a Frenchwoman, of truckling to the enemy. Jack Cade's rising and the murder of the Duke of Suffolk had been the outcome of this feeling. Indeed, Lord Salisbury's messenger reported the Country about London to be in so disturbed a state that it was no wonder that the Lady of Whitburn did not make the journey. She was not, as the Countess suspected, a very tender mother. Grisell's moans were far more frequently for her nurse than for her, but after some space they ceased. The child became capable of opening first one eye, then the other, and both barber and lady perceived that she was really unscathed in any vital part, and was on the way to recovery, though apparently with hopelessly injured features.

Leonard Copeland had already been released from

restraint, and allowed to resume his usual place among the Earl's pages; when the warder announced that he saw two parties approaching from opposite sides of the down, one as if from Salisbury, the other from the north; and presently he reported that the former wore the family badge, a white rosette, the latter none at all, whence it was perceived that the latter were adherents of the Beauforts of Somerset, for though the "Rose of Snow" had been already adopted by York, Somerset had in point of fact not plucked the Red Rose in the Temple gardens, nor was it as yet the badge of Lancaster.

Presently it was further reported that the Lady of Whitburn was in the fore front of the party, and the Lord of Salisbury hastened to receive her at the gates, his suite being rapidly put into some order.

She was a tall, rugged-faced North Country dame, not very smooth of speech, and she returned his salute with somewhat rough courtesy, demanding as she sprang off her horse with little aid, "Lives my wench still?"

"Yes, madam, she lives, and the leech trusts that she will yet be healed."

"Ah! Methought you would have sent to me if aught further had befallen her. Be that as it may, no doubt you have given the malapert boy his deserts."

"I hope I have, madam," began the Earl. "I kept him in close ward while she was in peril of death, but -" A fresh bugle blast interrupted him, as there clattered through the resounding gate the other troop, at sight of whom the Lady of Whitburn drew herself up, redoubling her grim dignity, and turning it into indignation as a young page rushed forward to meet the newcomers, with a cry of "Father! Lord Father, come at last;" then composing himself, doffed his cap and held the stirrup, then bent a knee for his father's blessing.

"You told me, Lord Earl, the mischievous, murderous fellow was in safe hold," said the lady, bending her dark brows.

"While the maid was in peril," hastily answered Salisbury. "Pardon me, madam, my Countess will attend you."

The Countess's high rank and great power were impressive to the Baroness of Whitburn, who bent in salutation, but almost her first words were, "Madam, you at least will not let the murderous traitors of Somerset and the Queen prevail over the loyal friends of York and the nation."

"There is happily no murder in the case. Praise be to the saints," said Countess Alice, "your little maid - "

"Aye, that's what they said as to the poor good Duke Humfrey," returned the irate lady; "but that you, madam, the good-sister of the noble York, should stand up for the enemies of him, and the friends of France, is more than a plain North Country woman like me can understand. And there - there, turning round upon the steep steps, there is my Lord Earl hand and glove with that minion fellow of Somerset, who was no doubt at the bottom of the plot! None would believe it at Raby."

"None at Raby would believe that my lord could be

lacking in courtesy to a guest," returned Lady Salisbury with dignity, "nor that a North Country dame could expect it of him. Those who are under his roof must respect it by fitting demeanour towards one another."

The Lady of Whitburn was quenched for the time, and the Countess asked whether she did not wish to see her daughter, leading the way to a chamber hung with tapestry, and with a great curtained bed nearly filling it up, for the patient had been installed in one of the best guest-chambers of the Castle. Lady Whitburn was surprised, but was too proud to show herself gratified by what she thought was the due of the dignity of the Dacres. An old woman in a hood sat by the bed, where there was a heap of clothes, and a dark-haired little girl stood by the window, whence she had been describing the arrivals in the Castle court.

"Here is your mother, my poor child," began the Lady of Salisbury, but there was no token of joy. Grisell gave a little gasp, and tried to say "Lady Mother, pardon - " but the Lady of Whitburn, at sight of the reddened half of the face which alone was as yet visible, gave a cry, "She will be a fright! You evil little baggage, thus to get yourself scarred and made hideous! Running where you ought not, I warrant!" and she put out her hand as if to shake the patient, but the Countess interposed, and her niece Margaret gave a little cry. "Grisell is still very weak and feeble! She cannot bear much; we have only just by Heaven's grace brought her round."

"As well she were dead as like this," cried this untender parent. "Who is to find her a husband now? and as to a nunnery, where is one to take her without a dower such as is hard to find, with two sons to be fitly provided? I looked that in a household like this, better rule should be kept."

"None can mourn it more than myself and the Earl," said the gentle Countess; "but young folks can scarce be watched hour by hour."

"The rod is all that is good for them, and I trusted to you to give it them, madam," said Lady Whitburn. "Now, the least that can be done is to force yonder malapert lad and his father into keeping his contract to her, since he has spoilt the market for any other."

"Is he contracted to her?" asked the Countess.

"Not fully; but as you know yourself, lady, your lord, and the King, and all the rest, thought to heal the breach between the houses by planning a contract between their son and my daughter. He shall keep it now, at his peril."

Grisell was cowering among her pillows, and no one knew how much she heard or understood. The Countess was glad to get Lady Whitburn out of the room, but both she and her Earl had a very trying evening, in trying to keep the peace between the two parents. Sir William Copeland was devoted to the Somerset family, of whom he held his manor; and had had a furious quarrel with the Baron of Whitburn, when both were serving in France.

The gentle King had tried to bring about a reconciliation, and had induced the two fathers to consent to a contract for the future marriage of Leonard, Copeland's second son, to Grisell Dacre, then the only child of the

Lord of Whitburn. He had also obtained that the two children should be bred up in the household of the Earl of Salisbury, by way of letting them grow up together. On the same principle the Lady of Whitburn had been made one of the attendants of Queen Margaret - but neither arrangement had been more successful than most of those of poor King Henry.

Grisell indeed considered Leonard as a sort of property of hers, but she beset him in the manner that boys are apt to resent from younger girls, and when he was thirteen, and she ten years old, there was very little affection on his side. Moreover, the birth of two brothers had rendered Grisell's hand a far less desirable prize in the eyes of the Copelands.

To attend on the Court was penance to the North Country dame, used to a hardy rough life in her sea-side tower, with absolute rule, and no hand over her save her husband's; while the young and outspoken Queen, bred up in the graceful, poetical Court of Aix or Nancy, looked on her as no better than a barbarian, and if she did not show this openly, reporters were not wanting to tell her that the Queen called her the great northern hag, or that her rugged unwilling curtsey was said to look as if she were stooping to draw water at a well. Her husband had kept her in some restraint, but when be had gone to Ireland with the Duke of York, offences seemed to multiply upon her. The last had been that when she had tripped on her train, dropped the salver wherewith she was serving the Queen, and broken out with a loud "Lawk a daisy!" all the ladies, and Margaret herself, had gone into fits of uncontrollable laughter, and the Queen had begged her to render her exclamation into good French for her benefit.

"Madam," she had exclaimed, "if a plain woman's plain English be not good enough for you, she can have no call here!" And without further ceremony she had flown out of the royal presence.

Margaret of Anjou, naturally offended, and never politic, had sent her a message, that her attendance was no longer required. So here she was going out of her way to make a casual inquiry, from the Court at Winchester, whether that very unimportant article, her only daughter, were dead or alive.

The Earl absolutely prohibited all conversation on affairs in debate during the supper which was spread in the hall, with quite as much state as, and even greater profusion and splendour, than was to be found at Windsor, Winchester, or Westminster. All the high born sat on the dais, raised on two steps with gorgeous tapestry behind, and a canopy overhead; the Earl and Countess on chairs in the centre of the long narrow table. Lady Whitburn sat beside the Earl, Sir William Copeland by the Countess, watching with pleasure how deftly his son ran about among the pages, carrying the trenchers of food, and the cups. He entered on a conversation with the Countess, telling her of the King's interest and delight in his beautiful freshly-founded Colleges at Eton and Cambridge, how the King rode down whenever he could to see the boys, listen to them at their tasks in the cloisters, watch them at their sports in the playing fields, and join in their devotions in the Chapel - a most holy example for them.

"Ay, for such as seek to be monks and shavelings," broke in the North Country voice sarcastically.

"There are others - sons of gentlemen and esquires - lodged in houses around," said Sir William, "who are not meant for cowl or for mass-priests."

"Yea, forsooth," called Lady Whitburn across the Earl and the Countess, "what for but to make them as feckless as the priests, unfit to handle lance or sword!"

"So, lady, you think that the same hand cannot wield pen and lance," said the Earl.

"I should like to see one of your clerks on a Border foray," laughed the Dame of Dacre. "'Tis all a device of the Frenchwoman!"

"Verily?" said the Earl, in an interrogative tone.

"Ay, to take away the strength and might of English-men with this clerkly lore, so that her folk may have the better of them in France; and the poor, witless King gives in to her. And so while the Beauforts rule the roast -"

Salisbury caught her up. "Ay, the roast. Will you partake of these roast partridges, madam?"

They were brought round skewered on a long spit, held by a page for the guest to help herself. Whether by her awkwardness or that of the boy, it so chanced that the bird made a sudden leap from the impalement, and deposited itself in the lap of Lady Whitburn's scarlet kirtle! The fact was proclaimed by her loud rude cry, "A murrain on thee, thou ne'er-do-weel lad," together with a sounding box on the ear.

"'Tis thine own greed, who dost not -"

"Leonard, be still - know thy manners," cried both at once the Earl and Sir William, for, unfortunately, the offender was no other than Leonard Copeland, and, contrary to all the laws of pagedom, he was too angry not to argue the point. "'Twas no doing of mine! She knew not how to cut the bird."

Answering again was a far greater fault than the first, and his father only treated it as his just desert when he was ordered off under the squire in charge to be soundly scourged, all the more sharply for his continuing to mutter, "It was her fault."

And sore and furrowed as was his back, he continued to exclaim, when his friend Edmund of York came to condole with him as usual in all his scrapes, "'Tis she that should have been scourged for clumsiness! A foul, uncouth Border dame! Well, one blessing at least is that now I shall never be wedded to her daughter - let the wench live or die as she lists!"

That was not by any means the opinion of the Lady of Whitburn, and no sooner was the meal ended than, in the midst of the hall, the debate began, the Lady declaring that in all honour Sir William Copeland was bound to affiance his son instantly to her poor daughter, all the more since the injuries he had inflicted to her face could never be done away with. On the other hand, Sir William Copeland was naturally far less likely to accept such a daughter-in-law, since her chances of being an heiress had ceased, and he contended that he had never absolutely accepted the contract, and that there had been no betrothal of the children.

The Earl of Salisbury could not but think that a strictly

honourable man would have felt poor Grisell's disaster inflicted by his son's hands all the more reason for holding to the former understanding; but the loud clamours and rude language of Lady Whitburn were enough to set any one in opposition to her, and moreover, the words he said in favour of her side of the question appeared to Copeland merely spoken out of the general enmity of the Nevils to the Beauforts and all their following.

Thus, all the evening Lady Whitburn raged, and appealed to the Earl, whose support she thought cool and unfriendly, while Copeland stood sullen and silent, but determined.

"My lord," she said, "were you a true friend to York and Raby, you would deal with this scowling fellow as we should on the Border."

"We are not on the Border, madam," quietly said Salisbury.

"But you are in your own Castle, and can force him to keep faith. No contract, forsooth! I hate your mincing South Country forms of law." Then perhaps irritated by a little ironical smile which Salisbury could not suppress. "Is this your castle, or is it not? Then bring him and his lad to my poor wench's side, and see their troth plighted, or lay him by the heels in the lowest cell in your dungeon. Then will you do good service to the King and the Duke of York, whom you talk of loving in your shilly-shally fashion."

"Madam," said the Earl, his grave tones coming in contrast to the shrill notes of the angry woman, "I counsel you, in the south at least, to have some respect to these same forms of law. I bid you a fair good-night. The chamberlain will marshal you."

CHAPTER III

THE MIRROR

"Of all the maids, the foulest maid
  From Teviot unto Dee.
Ah!" sighing said that lady then,
  "Can ne'er young Harden's be."

SCOTT, The Reiver's Wedding.

"They are gone," said Margaret of York, standing half dressed at the deep-set window of the chamber where Grisell lay in state in her big bed.

"Who are gone?" asked Grisell, turning as well as she could under the great heraldically-embroidered covering.

"Leonard Copeland and his father. Did'st not hear the horses' tramp in the court?"

"I thought it was only my lord's horses going to the water."

"It was the Copelands going off without breaking their fast or taking a stirrup cup, like discourteous rogues as they be," said Margaret, in no measured language.

"And are they gone? And wherefore?" asked Grisell.

"Wherefore? but for fear my noble uncle of Salisbury should hold them to their contract. Sir William sat as surly as a bear just about to be baited, while thy mother rated and raved at him like a very sleuth-hound on the chase. And Leonard - what think'st thou he saith? "That he would as soon wed the loathly lady as thee," the cruel Somerset villain as he is; and yet my brother Edmund is fain to love him. So off they are gone, like recreant curs as they are, lest my uncle should make them hear reason."

"But Lady Madge, dear Lady Madge, am I so very loathly?" asked poor Grisell.

"Mine aunt of Salisbury bade that none should tell thee," responded Margaret, in some confusion.

"Ah me! I must know sooner or later! My mother, she shrieked at sight of me!"

"I would not have your mother," said the outspoken daughter of "proud Cis." "My Lady Duchess mother is stern enough if we do not bridle our heads, and if we make ourselves too friendly with the meine, but she never frets nor rates us, and does not heed so long as we do not demean ourselves unlike our royal blood. She is no termagant like yours."

It was not polite, but Grisell had not seen enough of her mother to be very sensitive on her account. In fact, she was chiefly occupied with what she had heard about her own appearance - a matter which had not occurred to her before in all her suffering. She returned again to entreat Margaret to tell her whether she was so foully ill-favoured that no one could look at her, and the damsel of York, adhering to the letter rather young than the spirit of the cautions which she had received, pursed up her lips and reiterated that she had been commanded not to mention the subject.

"Then," entreated Grisell, "do - do, dear Madge - only bring me the little hand mirror out of my Lady Countess's chamber."

"I know not that I can or may."

"Only for the space of one Ave," reiterated Grisell.

"My lady aunt would never -"

"There - hark - there's the bell for mass. Thou canst run into her chamber when she and the tirewomen are gone down."

"But I must be there."

"Thou canst catch them up after. They will only think thee a slug-a-bed. Madge, dear Madge, prithee, I cannot rest without. Weeping will be worse for me."

She was crying, and caressing Margaret so vehemently that she gained her point. Indeed the other girl was afraid of her sobs being heard, and inquired into, and therefore promised to make the attempt, keeping a watch out of sight till she had seen the Lady of Salisbury in her padded head-gear of gold net, and long purple train, sweep down the stair, followed by her tirewomen and maidens of every degree. Then darting into the chamber, she bore away from a stage where lay the articles of the toilette, a little

Charlotte M. Yonge

silver-backed and handled Venetian mirror, with beautiful tracery in silvered glass diminishing the very small oval left for personal reflection and inspection. That, however, was quite enough and too much for poor Grisell when Lady Margaret had thrown it to her on her bed, and rushed down the stair so as to come in the rear of the household just in time.

A glance at the mirror disclosed, not the fair rosy face, set in light yellow curls, that Grisell had now and then peeped at in a bucket of water or a polished breast-plate, but a piteous sight. One half, as she expected, was hidden by bandages, but the other was fiery red, except that from the corner of the eye to the ear there was a purple scar; the upper lip was distorted, the hair, eyebrows, and lashes were all gone! The poor child was found in an agony of sobbing when, after the service, the old woman who acted as her nurse came stumping up in her wooden clogs to set the chamber and bed in order for Lady Whitburn's visit.

The dame was in hot haste to get home. Rumours were rife as to Scottish invasions, and her tower was not too far south not to need to be on its guard. Her plan was to pack Grisell on a small litter slung to a sumpter mule, and she snorted a kind of defiant contempt when the Countess, backed by the household barber-surgeon, declared the proceeding barbarous and impossible. Indeed she had probably forgotten that Grisell was far too tall to be made up into the bundle she intended; but she then declared that the wench might ride pillion behind old Diccon, and she would not be convinced till she was taken up to the sick chamber. There the first sound that greeted them was a choking agony of sobs and moans, while the tirewoman stood over the bed, exclaiming, "Aye, no wonder; it serves thee right, thou evil wench, filching my Lady Countess's mirror from her very chamber, when it might have been broken for all thanks to thee. The Venice glass that the merchant gave her! Thou art not so fair a sight, I trow, as to be in haste to see thyself. At the bottom of all the scathe in the Castle! We shall be well rid of thee."

So loud was the objurgation of the tirewoman that she did not hear the approach of her mistress, nor indeed the first words of the Countess, "Hush, Maudlin, the poor child is not to be thus rated! Silence!"

"See, my lady, what she has done to your ladyship's Venice glass, which she never should have touched. She must have run to your chamber while you were at mass. All false her feigning to be so sick and feeble."

"Ay," replied Lady Whitburn, "she must up - don her clothes, and away with me."

"Hush, I pray you, madam. How, how, Grisell, my poor child. Call Master Miles, Maudlin! Give me that water." The Countess was raising the poor child in her arms, and against her bosom, for the shock of that glance in the mirror, followed by the maid's harsh reproaches, and fright at the arrival of the two ladies, had brought on a choking, hysterical sort of convulsive fit, and the poor girl writhed and gasped on Lady Salisbury's breast, while her mother exclaimed, "Heed her not, Lady; it is all put on to hinder me from taking her home. If she could go stealing to your room -"

"No, no," broke out a weeping, frightened voice. "It was I, Lady Aunt. You bade me never tell her how her poor face looked, and when she begged and prayed me, I did not say, but I fetched the mirror. Oh! oh! It has not been the death of her."

"Nay, nay, by God's blessing! Take away the glass, Margaret. Go and tell thy beads, child; thou hast done much scathe unwittingly! Ah, Master Miles, come to the poor maid's aid. Canst do aught for her?"

"These humours must be drawn off, my lady," said the barber-surgeon, who advanced to the bed, and felt the pulse of the poor little patient. "I must let her blood."

Maudlin, whose charge she was, came to his help, and Countess Alice still held her up, while, after the practice of those days, he bled the already almost unconscious child, till she fainted and was laid down again on her pillows, under the keeping of Maudlin, while the clanging of the great bell called the family down to the meal which broke fast, whether to be called breakfast or dinner.

It was plain that Grisell was in no state to be taken on a journey, and her mother went grumbling down the stair at the unchancy bairn always doing scathe.

Lord Salisbury, beside whom she sat, courteously, though perhaps hardly willingly, invited her to remain till her daughter was ready to move.

"Nay, my Lord, I am beholden to you, but I may scarce do that. I be sorely needed at Whitburn Tower. The knaves go all agee when both my lord and myself have our backs turned, and my lad bairns - worth a dozen of yon whining maid - should no longer be left to old Cuthbert Ridley and Nurse. Now the Queen and Somerset have their way 'tis all misrule, and who knows what the Scots may do?"

"There are Nevils and Dacres enough between Whitburn and the Border," observed the Earl gravely. However, the visitor was not such an agreeable one as to make him anxious to press her stay beyond what hospitality demanded, and his wife could not bear to think of giving over her poor little patient to such usage as she would have met with on the journey.

Lady Whitburn was overheard saying that those who had mauled the maid might mend her, if they could; and accordingly she acquiesced, not too graciously, when the Countess promised to tend the child like her own, and send her by and by to Whitburn under a safe escort; and as Middleham Castle lay on the way to Whitburn, it was likely that means would be found of bringing or sending her.

This settled, Lady Whitburn was restless to depart, so as to reach a hostel before night.

She donned her camlet cloak and hood, and looked once more in upon Grisell, who after her loss of blood, had, on reviving, been made to swallow a draught of which an infusion of poppy heads formed a great part, so that she lay, breathing heavily, in a deep sleep, moaning now and then. Her mother did not scruple to try to rouse her with calls of "Grizzy! Look up, wench!" but could elicit nothing but a half turn on the pillow, and a little louder moan, and Master Miles, who was still watching, absolutely refused to let his patient be touched or shaken.

"Well a day!" said Lady Whitburn, softened for a moment, "what the Saints will must be, I trow; but it is hard, and I shall let St. Cuthbert of Durham know it, that after all the candles I have given him, he should have let my poor maid be so mauled and marred, and then forsaken by the rascal who did it, so that she will never be aught but a dead weight on my two fair sons! The least he can do for me now is to give me my revenge upon that lurdane runaway knight and his son. But he hath no care for lassies. Mayhap St. Hilda may serve me better."

Wherewith the Lady of Whitburn tramped down stairs. It may be feared that in the ignorance in which northern valleys were left she was very little more enlightened in her ideas of what would please the Saints, or what they could do for her, than were the old heathen of some unknown antiquity who used to worship in the mysterious circles of stones which lay on the downs of Amesbury.

CHAPTER IV

PARTING

There in the holy house at Almesbury
Weeping, none with her save a little maid.

TENNYSON, Idylls of the King.

The agitations of that day had made Grisell so much worse that her mind hardly awoke again to anything but present suffering from fever, and in consequence the aggravation of the wounds on her neck and cheek. She used to moan now and then "Don't take me away!" or cower in terror, "She is coming!" being her cry, or sometimes "So foul and loathly." She hung again between life and death, and most of those around thought death would be far better for the poor child, but the Countess and the Chaplain still held to the faith that she must be reserved for some great purpose if she survived so much.

Great families with all their train used to move from one castle or manor to another so soon as they had eaten up all the produce of one place, and the time had come when the Nevils must perforce quit Amesbury. Grisell was in no state for a long journey; she was exceedingly weak, and as fast as one wound in her face and neck healed another began to break out, so that

Charlotte M. Yonge

often she could hardly eat, and whether she would ever have the use of her left eye was doubtful.

Master Miles was at his wits' end, Maudlin was weary of waiting on her, and so in truth was every one except the good Countess, and she could not always be with the sufferer, nor could she carry such a patient to London, whither her lord was summoned to support his brother-in-law, the Duke of York, against the Duke of Somerset.

The only delay was caused by the having to receive the newly-appointed Bishop, Richard Beauchamp, who had been translated from his former see at Hereford on the murder of his predecessor, William Ayscough, by some of Jack Cade's party.

In full splendour he came, with a train of chaplains and cross-bearers, and the clergy of Salisbury sent a deputation to meet him, and to arrange with him for his reception and installation. It was then that the Countess heard that there was a nun at Wilton Abbey so skilled in the treatment of wounds and sores that she was thought to work miracles, being likewise a very holy woman.

The Earl and Countess would accompany the new bishop to be present at his enthronement and the ensuing banquet, and the lady made this an opportunity of riding to the convent on her way back, consulting the Abbess, whom she had long known, and likewise seeing Sister Avice, and requesting that her poor little guest might be received and treated there.

There was no chance of a refusal, for the great nobles were sovereigns in their own domains; the Countess owned half Wiltshire, and was much loved and honoured in all the religious houses for her devotion and beneficence.

The nuns were only too happy to undertake to receive the demoiselle Grisell Dacre of Whitburn, or any other whom my Lady Countess would entrust to them, and the Abbess had no doubt that Sister Avice could effect a cure.

Lady Salisbury dreaded that Grisell should lie awake all night crying, so she said nothing till her whirlicote, as the carriage of those days was called, was actually being prepared, and then she went to the chamber where the poor child had spent five months, and where she was now sitting dressed, but propped up on a sort of settle, and with half her face still bandaged.

"My little maid, this is well," said the Countess. "Come with me. I am going to take thee to a kind and holy dame who will, I trust, with the blessing of Heaven, be able to heal thee better than we have done."

"Oh, lady, lady, do not send me away!" cried Grisell; "not from you and Madge."

"My child, I must do so; I am going away myself, with my lord, and Madge is to go back with her brother to her father the Duke. Thou couldst not brook the journey, and I will take thee myself to the good Sister Avice."

"A nun, a nunnery," sighed Grisell. "Oh! I shall be mewed up there and never come forth again! Do not, I pray, do not, good my lady, send me thither!"

Perhaps my lady thought that to remain for life in a convent might be the fate, and perhaps the happiest, of the poor blighted girl, but she only told her that there was no reason she should not leave Wilton, as she was not put there to take the vows, but only to be cured.

Long nursing had made Grisell unreasonable, and she cried as much as she dared over the order; but no child ventured to make much resistance to elders in those days, and especially not to the Countess, so Grisell, a very poor little wasted being, was carried down, and only delayed in the hall for an affectionate kiss from Margaret of York.

"And here is a keepsake, Grisell," she said. "Mine own beauteous pouncet box, with the forget-me-nots in turquoises round each little hole."

"I will keep it for ever," said Grisell, and they parted, but not as girls part who hope to meet again, and can write letters constantly, but with tearful eyes and clinging hands, as little like to meet again, or even to hear more of one another.

The whirlicote was not much better than an ornamental waggon, and Lady Salisbury, with the Mother of the Maids, did their best to lessen the force of the jolts as by six stout horses it was dragged over the chalk road over the downs, passing the wonderful stones of Amesbury - a wider circle than even Stonehenge, though without the triliths, i.e. the stones laid one over the tops of the other two like a doorway. Grisell heard some thing murmured about Merlin and Arthur and Guinevere, but she did not heed, and she was quite worn out with fatigue by the time they reached the descent into the long smooth valley where Wilton

Abbey stood, and the spire of the Cathedral could be seen rising tall and beautiful.

The convent lay low, among meadows all shut in with fine elm trees, and the cows belonging to the sisters were being driven home, their bells tinkling. There was an outer court, within an arched gate kept by a stout porter, and thus far came the whirlicote and the Countess's attendants; but a lay porteress, in a cap and veil and black dress, came out to receive her as the door of the carriage was opened, and held out her arms to receive the muffled figure of the little visitor. "Ah, poor maid," she said, "but Sister Avice will soon heal her."

At the deeply ornamented round archway of the inner gate to the cloistered court stood the Lady Abbess, at the head of all her sisters, drawn up in double line to receive the Countess, whom they took to their refectory and to their chapel.

Of this, however, Grisell saw nothing, for she had been taken into the arms of a tall nun in a black veil. At first she shuddered and would have screamed if she had been a little stronger and less tired, for illness and weakness had brought back the babyish horror of anything black; but she felt soothed by the sweet voice and tender words, "Poor little one! she is fore spent. She shall lie down on a soft bed, and have some sweet milk anon."

Still a deadly feeling of faintness came upon her before she had been carried to the little bed which had been made ready for her. When she opened her eyes, while a spoon was held to her lips, the first thing she saw was the sweetest, calmest, most motherly of faces bent over

Charlotte M. Yonge

her, one arm round her, the other giving her the spoon of some cordial. She looked up and even smiled, though it was a sad contorted smile, which brought a tear into the good sister's eyes; but then she fell asleep, and only half awoke when the Countess came up to see her for the last time, and bade her farewell with a kiss on her forehead, and a charge to Sister Avice to watch her well, and be tender with her. Indeed no one could look at Sister Avice's gentle face and think there was much need of the charge.

Sister Avice was one of the women who seem to be especially born for the gentlest tasks of womanhood. She might have been an excellent wife and mother, but from the very hour of her birth she had been vowed to be a nun in gratitude on her mother's part for her father's safety at Agincourt. She had been placed at Wilton when almost a baby, and had never gone farther from it than on very rare occasions to the Cathedral at Salisbury; but she had grown up with a wonderful instinct for nursing and healing, and had a curious insight into the properties of herbs, as well as a soft deft hand and touch, so that for some years she had been sister infirmarer, and moreover the sick were often brought to the gates for her counsel, treatment, or, as some believed, even her healing touch.

When Grisell awoke she was alone in the long, large, low room, which was really built over the Norman cloister. The walls were of pale creamy stone, but at the end where she lay there were hangings of faded tapestry. At one end there was a window, through the thick glass of which could be dimly seen, as Grisell raised herself a little, beautiful trees, and the splendid spire of the Cathedral rising, as she dreamily thought, like a finger pointing upwards. Nearer were several more narrow windows along the side of the room, and that beside her bed had the lattice open, so that she saw a sloping green bank, with a river at the foot; and there was a trim garden between. Opposite to her there seemed to be another window with a curtain drawn across it, through which came what perhaps had wakened her, a low, clear murmuring tone, pausing and broken by the full, sweet, if rather shrill response in women's voices. Beneath that window was a little altar, with a crucifix and two candlesticks, a holy-water stoup by the side, and there was above the little deep window a carving of the Blessed Virgin with the Holy Child, on either side a niche, one with a figure of a nun holding a taper, the other of a bishop with a book.

Grisell might have begun crying again at finding herself alone, but the sweet chanting lulled her, and she lay back on her pillows, half dozing but quite content, except that the wound on her neck felt stiff and dry; and by and by when the chanting ceased, the kind nun, with a lay sister, came back again carrying water and other appliances, at sight of which Grisell shuddered, for Master Miles never touched her without putting her to pain.

"Benedicite, my little maid, thou art awake," said Sister Avice. "I thought thou wouldst sleep till the vespers were ended. Now let us dress these sad wounds of thine, and thou shalt sleep again."

Grisell submitted, as she knew she must, but to her surprise Sister Avice's touch was as soft and soothing as were her words, and the ointment she applied was fragrant and delicious and did not burn or hurt her.

Charlotte M. Yonge

She looked up gratefully, and murmured her thanks, and then the evening meal was brought in, and she sat up to partake of it on the seat of the window looking out on the Cathedral spire. It was a milk posset far more nicely flavoured than what she had been used to at Amesbury, where, in spite of the Countess's kindness, the master cook had grown tired of any special service for the Dacre wench; and unless Margaret of York secured fruit for her, she was apt to be regaled with only the scraps that Maudlin managed to cater for her after the meals were over.

After that, Sister Avice gently undressed her, took care that she said her prayers, and sat by her till she fell asleep, herself telling her that she should sleep beside her, and that she would hear the voices of the sisters singing in the chapel their matins and lauds. Grisell did hear them, as in a dream, but she had not slept so well since her disaster as she slept on that night.

CHAPTER V

SISTER AVICE

Love, to her ear, was but a name
Combined with vanity and shame;
Her hopes, her fears, her joys, were all
Bounded within the cloister wall.

SCOTT, Marmion.

Sister Avice sat in the infirmary, diligently picking the leaves off a large mass of wood-sorrel which had been brought to her by the children around, to make therewith a conserve.

Grisell lay on her couch. She had been dressed, and had knelt at the window, where the curtain was drawn back while mass was said by the Chaplain, the nuns kneeling in their order and making their responses. It was a low-browed chapel of Norman or even older days, with circular arches and heavy round piers, and so dark that the gleam of the candles was needed to light it.

Grisell watched, till tired with kneeling she went back to her couch, slept a little, and then wondered to see Sister Avice still compounding her simples.

She moved wearily, and sighed for Madge to come in and tell her all the news of Amesbury - who was riding at the ring, or who had shot the best bolt, or who had had her work picked out as not neat or well shaded enough.

Sister Avice came and shook up her pillow, and gave her a dried plum and a little milk, and began to talk to her.

"You will soon be better," she said, "and then you will be able to play in the garden."

"Is there any playfellow for me?" asked Grisell.

"There is a little maid from Bemerton, who comes daily to learn her hornbook and her sampler. Mayhap she will stay and play with you."

"I had Madge at Amesbury; I shall love no one as well as Madge! See what she gave me."

Grisell displayed her pouncet box, which was duly admired, and then she asked wearily whether she should always have to stay in the convent.

"Oh no, not of need," said the sister. "Many a maiden who has been here for a time has gone out into the world, but some love this home the best, as I have done."

"Did yonder nun on the wall?" asked Grisell.

"Yea, truly. She was bred here, and never left it, though she was a King's daughter. Edith was her name, and two days after Holy Cross day we shall keep her feast. Shall I tell you her story?"

"Prithee, prithee!" exclaimed Grisell. "I love a tale dearly."

Sister Avice told the legend, how St. Edith grew in love and tenderness at Wilton, and how she loved the gliding river and the flowers in the garden, and how all loved her, her young playmates especially. She promised one who went away to be wedded that she would be godmother to her first little daughter, but ere the daughter was born the saintly Edith had died. The babe was carried to be christened in the font at Winchester Cathedral, and by a great and holy man, no other than Alphegius, who was then Bishop of Winchester, but was made Archbishop of Canterbury, and died a holy martyr.

"Then," said Sister Avice, "there was a great marvel, for among the sponsors around the square black font there stood another figure in the dress of our Mother Abbess, and as the Bishop spake and said, "Bear this taper, in token that thy lamp shall be alight when the Bridegroom cometh," the form held the torch, shining bright, clear, and like no candle or light on earth ever shone, and the face was the face of the holy Edith. It is even said that she held the babe, but that I know not, being a spirit without a body, but she spake the name, her own name Edith. And when the holy rite was over, she had vanished away."

"And that is she, with the lamp in her hand? Oh, I should have been afraid!" cried Grisell.

"Not of the holy soul?" said the sister.

"Oh! I hope she will never come in here, by the little window into the church," cried Grisell trembling.

Indeed, for some time, in spite of all Sister Avice could say, Grisell could not at night be free from the fear of a visit from St. Edith, who, as she was told, slept her long sleep in the church below. It may be feared that one chief reliance was on the fact that she could not be holy enough for a vision of the Saint, but this was not so valuable to her as the touch of Sister Avice's kind hand, or the very knowing her present.

That story was the prelude to many more. Grisell wanted to hear it over again, and then who was the Archbishop martyr, and who were the Virgins in memory of whom the lamps were carried. Both these, and many another history, parable, or legend were told her by Sister Avice, training her soul, throughout the long recovery, which was still very slow, but was becoming more confirmed every day. Grisell could use her eye, turn her head, and the wounds closed healthily under the sister's treatment without showing symptoms of breaking out afresh; and she grew in strength likewise, first taking a walk in the trim garden and orchard, and by and by being pronounced able to join the other girl scholars of the convent. Only here was the first demur. Her looks did not recover with her health. She remained with a much-seamed neck, and a terrible scar across each cheek, on one side purple, and her eyebrows were entirely gone.

She seemed to have forgotten the matter while she was entirely in the infirmary, with no companion but Sister Avice, and occasionally a lay sister, who came to help; but the first time she went down the turret stair into the cloister - a beautiful succession of arches round a green court - she met a novice and a girl about her own age; the elder gave a little scream at the sight and ran away.

The other hung back. "Mary, come hither," said Sister Avice. "This is Grisell Dacre, who hath suffered so much. Wilt thou not come and kiss and welcome her?"

Mary came forward rather reluctantly, but Grisell drew up her head within, "Oh, if you had liefer not!" and turned her back on the girl.

Sister Avice followed as Grisell walked away as fast as her weakness allowed, and found her sitting breathless at the third step on the stairs.

"Oh, no - go away - don't bring her. Every one will hate me," sobbed the poor child.

Avice could only gather her into her arms, though embraces were against the strict rule of Benedictine nuns, and soothe and coax her to believe that by one at least she was not hated.

"I had forgotten," said Grisell. "I saw myself once at Amesbury! But my face was not well then. Let me see again, sister! Where's a mirror?"

"Ah! my child, we nuns are not allowed the use of worldly things like mirrors; I never saw one in my life."

"But oh, for pity's sake, tell me what like am I. Am I so loathly?"

"Nay, my dear maid, I love thee too well to think of aught save that thou art mine own little one, given back

Charlotte M. Yonge

to us by the will of Heaven. Aye, and so will others think of thee, if thou art good and loving to them."

"Nay, nay, none will ever love me! All will hate and flee from me, as from a basilisk or cockatrice, or the Loathly Worm of Spindlesheugh," sobbed Grisell.

"Then, my maid, thou must win them back by thy sweet words and kind deeds. They are better than looks. And here too they shall soon think only of what thou art, not of what thou look'st."

"But know you, sister, how - how I should have been married to Leonard Copeland, the very youth that did me this despite, and he is fair and beauteous as a very angel, and I did love him so, and now he and his father rid away from Amesbury, and left me because I am so foul to see," cried Grisell, between her sobs.

"If they could treat thee thus despiteously, he would surely not have made thee a good husband," reasoned the sister.

"But I shall never have a husband now," wailed Grisell.

"Belike not," said Sister Avice; "but, my sweetheart, there is better peace and rest and cheer in such a home as this holy house, than in the toils and labours of the world. When my sisters at Dunbridge and Dinton come to see me they look old and careworn, and are full of tales of the turmoil and trouble of husbands, and sons, and dues, and tenants' fees, and villeins, and I know not what, that I often think that even in this world's sense I am the best off. And far above and beyond that," she added, in a low voice , " the virgin hath a hope, a Spouse beyond all human thought."

Grisell did not understand the thought, and still wept bitterly. "Must she be a nun all her life?" was all she thought of, and the shady cloister seemed to her like a sort of prison. Sister Avice had to soothe and comfort her, till her tears were all spent, as so often before, and she had cried herself so ill that she had to be taken back to her bed and lie down again. It was some days before she could be coaxed out again to encounter any companions.

However, as time went on, health, and with it spirits and life, came back to Grisell Dacre at Wilton, and she became accustomed to being with the other inmates of the fine old convent, as they grew too much used to her appearance to be startled or even to think about it. The absence of mirrors prevented it from ever being brought before her, and Sister Avice set herself to teach her how goodness, sweetness, and kindness could endear any countenance, and indeed Grisell saw for herself how much more loved was the old and very plain Mother Anne than the very beautiful young Sister Isabel, who had been forced into the convent by her tyrannical brother, and wore out her life in fretting and rudeness to all who came in her way. She declared that the sight of Grisell made her ill, and insisted that the veiled hood which all the girls wore should be pulled forward whenever they came near one another, and that Grisell's place should be out of her sight in chapel or refectory.

Every one else, however, was very kind to the poor girl, Sister Avice especially so, and Grisell soon forgot her disfigurement when she ceased to suffer from it. She had begun to learn reading, writing, and a little

Charlotte M. Yonge

Latin, besides spinning, stitchery, and a few house-wifely arts, in the Countess of Salisbury's household, for every lady was supposed to be educated in these arts, and great establishments were schools for the damsels there bred up. It was the same with convent life, and each nunnery had traditional works of its own, either in embroidery, cookery, or medicine. Some secrets there were not imparted beyond the professed nuns, and only to the more trustworthy of them, so that each sisterhood might have its own especial glory in confections, whether in portrait-worked vestments, in illuminations, in sweetmeats, or in salves and unguents; but the pensioners were instructed in all those common arts of bakery, needlework, notability, and surgery which made the lady of a castle or manor so important, and within the last century in the more fashionable abbeys Latin of a sort, French "of the school of Stratford le Bowe," and the like, were added. Thus Grisell learnt as an apt scholar these arts, and took especial delight in helping Sister Avice to compound her simples, and acquired a tender hand with which to apply them.

Moreover, she learnt not only to say and sing her Breviary, but to know the signification in English. There were translations of the Lord's Prayer and Creed in the hands of all careful and thoughtful people, even among the poor, if they had a good parish priest, or had come under the influence of the better sort of friars. In convents where discipline was kept up the meaning was carefully taught, and there were English primers in the hands of all the devout, so that the services could be intelligently followed even by those who did not learn Latin, as did Grisell. Selections from Scripture history, generally clothed in rhyme, and versified lives of the Saints, were read aloud at meal-times in the refectory, and Grisell became so good a reader that she was often chosen to chant out the sacred story, and her sweet northern voice was much valued in the singing in the church. She was quite at home there, and though too young to be admitted as a novice, she wore a black dress and white hood like theirs, and the annual gifts to the nunnery from the Countess of Salisbury were held to entitle her to the residence there as a pensioner. She had fully accepted the idea of spending her life there, sheltered from the world, among the kind women whom she loved, and who had learnt to love her, and in devotion to God, and works of mercy to the sick.

CHAPTER VI

THE PROCTOR

But if a mannes soul were in his purse,
For in his purse he should yfurnished be.

CHAUCER, Canterbury Pilgrims.

Five years had passed since Grisell had been received at Wilton, when the Abbess died. She had been infirm and confined to her lodging for many months, and Grisell had hardly seen her, but her death was to change the whole tenor of the maiden's life.

The funeral ceremonies took place in full state. The Bishop himself came to attend them, and likewise all the neighbouring clergy, and the monks, friars, and nuns, overflowing the chapel, while peasants and beggars for whom there was no room in the courts encamped outside the walls, to receive the dole and pray for the soul of the right reverend Mother Abbess.

For nine days constant services were kept up, and the requiem mass was daily said, the dirges daily sung, and the alms bestowed on the crowd, who were by no means specially sorrowful or devout, but beguiled the time by watching jongleurs and mountebanks performing beyond the walls.

There was the "Month's Mind" still to come, and then the chapter of nuns intended to proceed to the election of their new Abbess, unanimously agreeing that she should be their present Prioress, who had held kindly rule over them through the slow to-decay of the late Abbess. Before, however, this could be done a messenger arrived on a mule bearing an inhibition to the sisters to proceed in the election.

His holiness Pope Calixtus had reserved to himself the next appointment to this as well as to certain other wealthy abbeys.

The nuns in much distress appealed to the Bishop, but he could do nothing for them. Such reservations had been constant in the subservient days that followed King John's homage, and though the great Edwards had struggled against them, and the yoke had been shaken off during the Great Schism, no sooner had this been healed than the former claims were revived, nay, redoubled, and the pious Henry VI. was not the man to resist them. The sisters therefore waited in suspense, daring only meekly to recommend their Prioress in a humble letter, written by the Chaplain, and backed by a recommendation from Bishop Beauchamp. Both alike were disregarded, as all had expected.

The new Abbess thus appointed was the Madre Matilda de Borgia, a relation of Pope Calixtus, very noble, and of Spanish birth, as the Commissioner assured the nuns; but they had never heard of her before, and were not at all gratified. They had always elected their Abbess before, and had quite made up their minds as to the choice of the present Mother Prioress as Abbess, and of Sister Avice as Prioress.

However, they had only to submit. To appeal to the King or to their Bishop would have been quite useless; they could only do as the Pope commanded, and elect the Mother Matilda, consoling themselves with the reflection that she was not likely to trouble herself about them, and their old Prioress would govern them. And so she did so far as regarded the discipline of the house, but what they had not so entirely understood was the Mother de Borgia's desire to squeeze all she could out of the revenues of the house.

Her Proctor arrived, a little pinched man in a black gown and square cap, and desired to see the Mother Prioress and her steward, and to overlook the income and expenditure of the convent; to know who had duly paid her dowry to the nunnery, what were the rents, and the like. The sisters had already raised a considerable gift in silver merks to be sent through Lombard merchants to their new Abbess, and this requisition was a fresh blow.

Presently the Proctor marked out Grisell Dacre, and asked on what terms she was at the convent. It was explained that she had been brought thither for her cure by the Lady of Salisbury, and had stayed on, without fee or payment from her own home in the north, but the ample donations of the Earl of Salisbury had been held as full compensation, and it had been contemplated to send to the maiden's family to obtain permission to enrol her as a sister after her novitiate - which might soon begin, as she was fifteen years old.

The Proctor, however, was much displeased. The nuns had no right to receive a pensioner without payment, far less to admit a novice as a sister without a dowry.

Mistress Grisell must be returned instantly upon the hands either of her own family or of the Countess of Salisbury, and certainly not readmitted unless her dowry were paid. He scarcely consented to give time for communication with the Countess, to consider how to dispose of the poor child.

The Prioress sent messengers to Amesbury and to Christ Church, but the Earl and Countess were not there, nor was it clear where they were likely to be. Whitburn was too far off to send to in the time allowed by the Proctor, and Grisell had heard nothing from her home all the time she had been at Wilton. The only thing that the Prioress could devise, was to request the Chaplain to seek her out at Salisbury a trustworthy escort, pilgrim, merchant or other, with whom Grisell might safely travel to London, and if the Earl and Countess were not there, some responsible person of theirs, or of their son's, was sure to be found, who would send the maiden on.

The Chaplain mounted his mule and rode over to Salisbury, whence he returned, bringing with him news of a merchant's wife who was about to go on pilgrimage to fulfil a vow at Walsingham, and would feel herself honoured by acting as the convoy of the Lady Grisell Dacre as far at least as London.

There was no further hope of delay or failure. Poor Grisell must be cast out on the world - the Proctor even spoke of calling the Countess, or her steward, to account for her maintenance during these five years.

There was weeping and wailing in the cloisters at the parting, and Grisell clung to Sister Avice, mourning for her peaceful, holy life.

"Nay, my child, none can take from thee a holy life."

"If I make a vow of virginity none can hinder me."

"That was not what I meant. No maid has a right to take such a vow on herself without consent of her father, nor is it binding otherwise. No! but no one can take away from a Christian maid the power of holiness. Bear that for ever in mind, sweetheart. Naught that can be done by man or by devil to the body can hurt the soul that is fixed on Christ and does not consent to evil."

"The Saints forefend that ever - ever I should consent to evil."

"It is the Blessed Spirit alone who can guard thy will, my child. Will and soul not consenting nor being led astray thou art safe. Nay, the lack of a fair-favoured face may be thy guard."

"All will hate me. Alack! alack!"

"Not so. See, thou hast won love amongst us. Wherefore shouldst not thou in like manner win love among thine own people?"

"My mother hates me already, and my father heeds me not."

"Love them, child! Do them good offices! None can hinder thee from that."

"Can I love those who love not me?"

"Yea, little one. To serve and tend another brings the

heart to love. Even as thou seest a poor dog love the master who beats him, so it is with us, only with the higher Christian love. Service and prayer open the heart to love, hoping for nothing again, and full oft that which was not hoped for is vouchsafed."

That was the comfort with which Grisell had to start from her home of peace, conducted by the Chaplain, and even the Prioress, who would herself give her into the hands of the good Mistress Hall.

Very early they heard mass in the convent, and then rode along the bank of the river, with the downs sloping down on the other side, and the grand spire ever seeming as it were taller as they came nearer; while the sound of the bells grew upon them, for there was then a second tower beyond to hold the bells, whose reverberation would have been dangerous to the spire, and most sweet was their chime, the sound of which had indeed often reached Wilton in favourable winds; but it sounded like a sad farewell to Grisell.

The Prioress thought she ought to begin her journey by kneeling in the Cathedral, so they crossed the shaded close and entered by the west door with the long vista of clustered columns and pointed arches before them.

Low sounds of mass being said at different altars met their ears, for it was still early in the day. The Prioress passed the length of nave, and went beyond the choir to the lady chapel, with its slender supporting columns and exquisite arches, and there she, with Grisell by her side, joined in earnest supplications for the child.

The Chaplain touched her as she rose, and made her aware that the dame arrayed in a scarlet mantle and hood and dark riding-dress was Mistress Hall.

Silence was not observed in cathedrals or churches, especially in the naves, except when any sacred rite was going on, and no sooner was the mass finished and "Ite missa est" pronounced than the scarlet cloak rose, and hastened into the south transept, where she waited for the Chaplain, Prioress, and Grisell. No introduction seemed needed. "The Holy Mother Prioress," she began, bending her knee and kissing the lady's hand. "Much honoured am I by the charge of this noble little lady." Grisell by the by was far taller than the plump little goodwoman Hall, but that was no matter, and the Prioress had barely space to get in a word of thanks before she went on: "I will keep her and tend her as the apple of mine eye. She shall pray with me at all the holy shrines for the good of her soul and mine. She shall be my bedfellow wherever we halt, and sit next me, and be cherished as though she were mine own daughter - ladybird as she is - till I can give her into the hands of the good Lady Countess. Oh yes - you may trust Joan Hall, dame reverend mother. She is no new traveller. I have been in my time to all our shrines - to St. Thomas of Canterbury, to St. Winifred's Well, aye, and, moreover, to St. James of Compostella, and St. Martha of Provence, not to speak of lesser chantries and Saints. Aye, and I crossed the sea to see the holy coat of Treves, and St. Ursula's eleven thousand skulls - and a gruesome sight they were. Nay, if the Lady Countess be not in London it would cost me little to go on to the north with her. There's St. Andrew of Ely, Hugh, great St. Hugh and little St. Hugh, both of them at Lincoln, and there's St. Wilfred of York, and St. John of Beverly, not to speak of St. Cuthbert of Durham and of St. Hilda of Whitby, who might take it ill if I pray at none of their altars, when I have been to so many of their brethren. Oh, you may trust me, reverend mother; I'll never have the young lady, bless her sweet face, out of my sight till I have safe bestowed her with my Lady Countess, our good customer for all manner of hardware, or else with her own kin."

The good woman's stream of conversation lasted almost without drawing breath all the way down the nave. It was a most good-humoured hearty voice, and her plump figure and rosy face beamed with good nature, while her bright black eyes had a lively glance.

The Chaplain had inquired about her, and found that she was one of the good women to whom pilgrimage was an annual dissipation, consecrated and meritorious as they fondly believed, and gratifying their desire for change and variety. She was a kindly person of good reputation, trustworthy, and kind to the poor, and stout John Hall, her husband, could manage the business alone, and was thought not to regret a little reprieve from her continual tongue.

She wanted the Prioress to do her the honour of breaking her fast with her, but the good nun was in haste to return, after having once seen her charge in safe hands, and excused herself, while Grisell, blessed by the Chaplain, and hiding her tears under her veil, was led away to the substantial smith's abode, where she was to take a first meal before starting on her journey on the strong forest pony which the Chaplain's care had provided for her.

Charlotte M. Yonge

CHAPTER VII

THE PILGRIM OF SALISBURY

She hadde passed many a strange shrine,
At Rome she had been and at Boleine,
At Galice, at St. James, and at Coleine,
She could moche of wandering by the way.

CHAUCER, Canterbury Pilgrims.

Grisell found herself brought into a hall where a stout oak table occupied the centre, covered with home-spun napery, on which stood trenchers, wooden bowls, pewter and a few silver cups, and several large pitchers of ale, small beer, or milk. A pie and a large piece of bacon, also a loaf of barley bread and a smaller wheaten one, were there.

Shelves all round the walls shone with pewter and copper dishes, cups, kettles, and vessels and implements of all household varieties, and ranged round the floor lay ploughshares, axes, and mattocks, all polished up. The ring of hammers on the anvil was heard in the court in the rear. The front of the hall was open for the most part, without windows, but it could be closed at night.

Breakfast was never a regular meal, and the household

had partaken of it, so that there was no one in the hall excepting Master Hall, a stout, brawny, grizzled man, with a good-humoured face, and his son, more slim, but growing into his likeness, also a young notable-looking daughter-in-law with a swaddled baby tucked under her arm.

They seated Grisell at the table, and implored her to eat. The wheaten bread and the fowl were, it seemed, provided in her honour, and she could not but take her little knife from the sheath in her girdle, turn back her nun-like veil, and prepare to try to drive back her sobs, and swallow the milk of almonds pressed on her.

"Eh!" cried the daughter-in-law in amaze. "She's only scarred after all."

"Well, what else should she be, bless her poor heart?" said Mrs. Hall the elder.

"Why, wasn't it thou thyself, good mother, that brought home word that they had the pig-faced lady at Wilton there?"

"Bless thee, Agnes, thou should'st know better than to lend an ear to all the idle tales thy poor old mother may hear at market or fair."

"Then should we have enough to do," muttered her husband.

"And as thou seest, 'tis a sweet little face, only cruelly marred by the evil hap."

Poor Grisell was crimson at finding all eyes on her, an ordeal she had never undergone in the convent, and she

Charlotte M. Yonge

hastily pulled forward her veil.

"Nay now, my sweet young lady, take not the idle words in ill part," pleaded the good hostess. "We all know how to love thee, and what is a smooth skin to a true heart? Take a bit more of the pasty, ladybird; we'll have far to ride ere we get to Wherwell, where the good sisters will give us a meal for young St. Edward's sake and thy Prioress's. Aye - I turn out of my way for that; I never yet paid my devotion to poor young King Edward, and he might take it in dudgeon, being a king, and his shrine so near at hand."

"Ha, ha!" laughed the smith; "trust my dame for being on the right side of the account with the Saints. Well for me and Jack that we have little Agnes here to mind the things on earth meanwhile. Nay, nay, dame, I say nought to hinder thee; I know too well what it means when spring comes, and thou beginn'st to moan and tell up the tale of the shrines where thou hast not told thy beads."

It was all in good humour, and Master Hall walked out to the city gate to speed his gad-about or pious wife, whichever he might call her, on her way, apparently quite content to let her go on her pilgrimages for the summer quarter.

She rode a stout mule, and was attended by two sturdy varlets - quite sufficient guards for pilgrims, who were not supposed to carry any valuables. Grisell sadly rode her pony, keeping her veil well over her face, yearning over the last view of the beloved spire, thinking of Sister Avice ministering to her poor, and with a very definite fear of her own reception in the world and dread of her welcome at home. Yet there was a joy in being on horseback once more, for her who had ridden moorland ponies as soon as she could walk.

Goodwife Hall talked on, with anecdotes of every hamlet that they passed, and these were not very many. At each church they dismounted and said their prayers, and if there were a hostel near, they let their animals feed the while, and obtained some refreshment themselves. England was not a very safe place for travellers just then, but the cockle-shells sewn to the pilgrim's hat of the dame, and to that of one of her attendants, and the tall staff and wallet each carried, were passports of security. Nothing could be kinder than Mistress Hall was to her charge, of whom she was really proud, and when they halted for the night at the nunnery of Queen Elfrida at Wherwell, she took care to explain that this was no burgess's daughter but the Lady Grisell Dacre of Whitburn, trusted to HER convoy, and thus obtained for her quarters in the guest-chamber of the refectory instead of in the general hospitium; but on the whole Grisell had rather not have been exposed to the shock of being shown to strangers, even kindly ones, for even if they did not exclaim, some one was sure to start and whisper.

After another halt for the night the travellers reached London, and learned at the city gate that the Earl and Countess of Salisbury were absent, but that their eldest son, the Earl of Warwick, was keeping court at Warwick House.

Thither therefore Mistress Hall resolved to conduct Grisell. The way lay through narrow streets with houses overhanging the roadway, but the house itself was like a separate castle, walled round, enclosing a huge space, and with a great arched porter's lodge, where various men-at-arms lounged, all adorned on the arm of their red jackets with the bear and ragged staff.

They were courteous, however, for the Earl Richard of Warwick insisted on civility to all comers, and they respected the scallop-shell on the dame's hat. They greeted her good-humouredly.

"Ha, good-day, good pilgrim wife. Art bound for St. Paul's? Here's supper to the fore for all comers!"

"Thanks, sir porter, but this maid is of other mould; she is the Lady Grisell Dacre, and is company for my lord and my lady."

"Nay, her hood and veil look like company for the Abbess. Come this way, dame, and we will find the steward to marshal her."

Grisell had rather have been left to the guardianship of her kind old friend, but she was obliged to follow. They dismounted in a fine court with cloister-like buildings round it, and full of people of all kinds, for no less than six hundred stout yeomen wore red coats and the bear and ragged staff. Grisell would fain have clung to her guide, but she was not allowed to do so. She was marshalled up stone steps into a great hall, where tables were being laid, covered with white napery and glittering with silver and pewter.

The seneschal marched before her all the length of the hall to where there was a large fireplace with a burning log, summer though it was, and shut off by handsome tapestried and carved screens sat a half circle of ladies, with a young-looking lady in a velvet fur-trimmed surcoat in their midst. A tall man with a keen, resolute face, in long robes and gold belt and chain, stood by her leaning on her chair.

The seneschal announced, "Place, place for the Lady Grisell Dacre of Whitburn," and Grisell bent low, putting back as much of her veil as she felt courtesy absolutely to require. The lady rose, the knight held out his hand to raise the bending figure. He had that power of recollection and recognition which is so great an element in popularity. "The Lady Grisell Dacre," he said. "She who met with so sad a disaster when she was one of my lady mother's household?"

Grisell glowing all over signed acquiescence, and he went on, "Welcome to my poor house, lady. Let me present you to my wife."

The Countess of Warwick was a pale, somewhat inane lady. She was the heiress of the Beauchamps and De Spensers in consequence of the recent death of her brother, "the King of the Isle of Wight" - and through her inheritance her husband had risen to his great power. She was delicate and feeble, almost apathetic, and she followed her husband's lead, and received her guest with fair courtesy; and Grisell ventured in a trembling voice to explain that she had spent those years at Wilton, but that the new Abbess's Proctor would not consent to her remaining there any longer, not even long enough to send to her parents or to the Countess of Salisbury.

"Poor maiden! Such are the ways of his Holiness where the King is not man enough to stand in his way," said Warwick. "So, fair maiden, if you will honour my house for a few days, as my lady's guest, I will send you north in more fitting guise than with this white-smith dame."

"She hath been very good to me," Grisell ventured to add to her thanks.

"She shall have good entertainment here," said the Earl smiling. "No doubt she hath already, as Sarum born. See that Goodwife Hall, the white smith's wife, and her following have the best of harbouring," he added to his silver-chained steward.

"You are a Dacre of Whitburn," he added to Grisell. "Your father has not taken sides with Dacre of Gilsland and the Percies." Then seeing that Grisell knew nothing of all this, he laughed and said, "Little convent birds, you know nought of our worldly strifes."

In fact, Grisell had heard nothing from her home for the last five years, which was the less marvel as neither her father nor her mother could write if they had cared to do so. Nor did the convent know much of the state of England, though prayers had been constantly said for the King's recovery, and of late there had been thanksgivings for the birth of the Prince of Wales; but it was as much as she did know that just now the Duke of York was governing, for the poor King seemed as senseless as a stone, and the Earl of Salisbury was his Chancellor. Nevertheless Salisbury was absent in the north, and there was a quarrel going on between the Nevils and the Percies which Warwick was going to compose, and thus would be able to take Grisell so far in his company.

The great household was larger than even what she remembered at the houses of the Countess of Salisbury before her accident, and, fresh from the stillness of the convent as she was, the noises were amazing to her when all sat down to supper. Tables were laid all along the vast hall. She was placed at the upper one to her relief, beside an old lady, Dame Gresford, whom she remembered to have seen at Montacute Castle in her childhood, as one of the attendants on the Countess. She was forced to put back her veil, and she saw some of the young knights and squires staring at her, then nudging one another and laughing.

"Never mind them, sweetheart," said Dame Gresford kindly; "they are but unmannerly lurdanes, and the Lord Earl would make them know what is befitting if his eye fell on them."

The good lady must have had a hint from the authorities, for she kept Grisell under her wing in the huge household, which was like a city in itself. There was a knight who acted as steward, with innumerable knights, squires, and pages under him, besides the six hundred red jacketed yoemen, and servants of all degrees, in the immense court of the buttery and kitchen, as indeed there had need to be, for six oxen were daily cooked, with sheep and other meats in proportion, and any friend or acquaintance of any one in this huge establishment might come in, and not only eat and drink his fill, but carry off as much meat as he could on the point of his dagger.

Goodwife Hall, as coming from Salisbury, stayed there in free quarters, while she made the round of all the shrines in London, and she was intensely gratified by the great Earl recollecting, or appearing to recollect, her and inquiring after her husband, that hearty burgess, whose pewter was so lasting, and he was sure was still in use among his black guard.

When she saw Grisell on finally departing for St. Albans, she was carrying her head a good deal higher on the strength of "my Lord Earl's grace to her." She hoped that her sweet Lady Grisell would remain here, as the best hap she could have in the most noble, excellent, and open-handed house in the world! Grisell's own wishes were not the same, for the great household was very bewildering - a strange change from her quietly-busy convent. The Countess was quiet enough, but dull and sickly, and chiefly occupied by her ailments. She seemed to be always thinking about leeches, wise friars, wonderful nuns, or even wizards and cunning women, and was much concerned that her husband absolutely forbade her consulting the witch of Spitalfields.

"Nay, dame," said he, "an thou didst, the next thing we should hear would be that thou hadst been sticking pins into King Harry's waxen image and roasting him before the fire, and that nothing but roasting thee in life and limb within a fire would bring him to life and reason."

"They would never dare," cried the lady.

"Who can tell what the Queen would dare if she gets her will!" demanded the Earl. "Wouldst like to do penance with sheet and candle, like Gloucester's wife?"

Such a possibility was enough to silence the Lady of Warwick on the score of witches, and the only time she spoke to Grisell was to ask her about Sister Avice and her cures. She set herself to persuade her husband to let her go down to one of his mother's Wiltshire houses to consult the nun, but Warwick had business in the north, nor would he allow her to be separated from him, lest she might be detained as a hostage.

Dame Gresford continued to be Grisell's protector, and let the girl sit and spin or embroider beside her, while the other ladies of the house played at ball in the court, or watched the exercises of the pages and squires. The dame's presence and authority prevented Grisell's being beset with uncivil remarks, but she knew she was like a toad among the butterflies, as she overheard some saucy youth calling her, while a laugh answered him, and she longed for her convent.

CHAPTER VIII

OLD PLAYFELLOWS

Alone thou goest forth,
Thy face unto the north,
Moor and pleasance all around thee and beneath thee.

E. BARRETT BROWNING, A Valediction.

One great pleasure fell to Grisell's share, but only too brief. The family of the Duke of York on their way to Baynard's Castle halted at Warwick House, and the Duchess Cecily, tall, fair, and stately, sailed into the hall, followed by three fair daughters, while Warwick, her nephew, though nearly of the same age, advanced with his wife to meet and receive her.

In the midst of the exchange of affectionate but formal greetings a cry of joy was heard, "My Grisell! yes, it is my Grisell!" and springing from the midst of her mother's suite, Margaret Plantagenet, a tall, lovely, dark-haired girl, threw her arms round the thin slight maiden with the scarred face, which excited the scorn and surprise of her two sisters.

"Margaret! What means this?" demanded the Duchess severely.

"It is my Grisell Dacre, fair mother, my dear companion at my aunt of Salisbury's manor," said Margaret, trying to lead forward her shrinking friend. "She who was so cruelly scathed."

Grisell curtsied low, but still hung back, and Lord Warwick briefly explained. "Daughter to Will Dacre of Whitburn, a staunch baron of the north. My mother bestowed her at Wilton, whence the creature of the Pope's intruding Abbess has taken upon him to expel her. So I am about to take her to Middleham, where my mother may see to her further bestowal."

"We have even now come from Middleham," said the Duchess. "My Lord Duke sent for me, but he looks to you, my lord, to compose the strife between your father and the insolent Percies."

The Duke was at Windsor with the poor insane King, and the Earl and the Duchess plunged into a discussion of the latest news of the northern counties and of the Court. The elder daughters were languidly entertained by the Countess, but no one disturbed the interview of Margaret and Grisell, who, hand in hand, had withdrawn into the embrasure of a window, and there fondled each other, and exchanged tidings of their young lives, and Margaret told of friends in the Nevil household.

All too soon the interview came to an end. The Duchess, after partaking of a manchet, was ready to proceed to Baynard's Castle, and the Lady Margaret was called for. Again, in spite of surprised, not to say displeased looks, she embraced her dear old playfellow. "Don't go into a convent, Grisell," she entreated. "When I am wedded to some great earl, you must come and be my lady, mine own, own dear friend. Promise me! Your pledge, Grisell."

There was no time for the pledge. Margaret was peremptorily summoned. They would not meet again. The Duchess's intelligence had quickened Warwick's departure, and the next day the first start northwards was to be made.

It was a mighty cavalcade. The black guard, namely, the kitchen menage, with all their pots and pans, kettles and spits, were sent on a day's march beforehand, then came the yeomen, the knights and squires, followed by the more immediate attendants of the Earl and Countess and their court. She travelled in a whirlicote, and there were others provided for her elder ladies, the rest riding singly or on pillions according to age or taste. Grisell did not like to part with her pony, and Dame Gresford preferred a pillion to the bumps and jolts of the waggon-like conveyances called chariots, so Grisell rode by her side, the fresh spring breezes bringing back the sense of being really a northern maid, and she threw back her veil whenever she was alone with the attendants, who were used to her, though she drew it closely round when she encountered town or village. There were resting-places on the way. In great monasteries all were accommodated, being used to close quarters; in castles there was room for the "Gentles," who, if they fared well, heeded little how they slept, and their attendants found lairs in the kitchens or stables. In towns there was generally harbour for the noble portion; indeed in some, Warwick had dwellings of his own, or his father's, but these, at first, were at long distances apart, such as would be ridden by horsemen alone, not encumbered with ladies, and there were intermediate stages, where some of the party had to be dispersed in hostels.

It was in one of these, at Dunstable, that Dame Gresford had taken Grisell, and there were also sundry of the gentlemen of the escort. A minstrel was esconced under the wide spread of the chimney, and began to sound his harp and sing long ballads in recitative to the company. Whether he did it in all innocence and ignorance, or one of the young squires had mischievously prompted him, there was no knowing; Dame Gresford suspected the latter, when he began the ballad of "Sir Gawaine's Wedding." She would have silenced it, but feared to draw more attention on her charge, who had never heard the song, and did not know what was coming, but listened with increasing eagerness as she heard of King Arthur, and of the giant, and the secret that the King could not guess, till as he rode -

He came to the green forest,
      Underneath a green hollen tree,
There sat that lady in red scarlet
      That unseemly was to see.

Some eyes were discourteously turned on the maiden, but she hardly saw them, and at any rate her nose was not crooked, nor had her eyes and mouth changed places, as in the case of the "Loathly Lady." She heard of the condition on which the lady revealed the secret, and how King Arthur bound himself to bring a fair young knight to wed the hideous being. Then when he revealed to his assembled knights -

Then some took up their hawks,

And some took up their hounds,
And some sware they would not marry her
            For cities nor for towns.

Glances again went towards the scarred visage, but
Grisell was heedless of them, only listening how Sir
Gawaine, Arthur's nephew, felt that his uncle's oath
must be kept, and offered himself as the bridegroom.

Then after the marriage, when he looked on the lady,
instead of the loathly hag he beheld a fair damsel! And
he was told by her that he might choose whether she
should be foul at night and fair by day, or fair each
evening and frightful in the daylight hours. His choice
at first was that her beauty should be for him alone, in
his home, but when she objected that this would be
hard on her, since she could thus never show her face
when other dames ride with their lords -

Then buke him gentle Gawayne,
            Said, "Lady, that's but a shill;
Because thou art mine own lady
            Thou shalt have all thy will."

And his courtesy broke the spell of the stepdame, as
the lady related -

"She witched me, being a fair young lady,
            To the green forest to dwell,
And there must I walk in woman's likeness,
            Most like a fiend in hell."

Thenceforth the enchantment was broken, and Sir Gawaine's bride was fair to see.

Grisell had listened intently, absorbed in the narrative, so losing personal thought and feeling that it was startling to her to perceive that Dame Gresford was trying to hush a rude laugh, and one of the young squires was saying, "Hush, hush! for very shame."

Then she saw that they were applying the story to her, and the blood rushed into her face, but the more courteous youth was trying to turn away attention by calling on the harper for "The Beggar of Bethnal Green," or "Lord Thomas and Fair Annet," or any merry ballad. So it was borne in on Grisell that to these young gentlemen she was the lady unseemly to see. Yet though a few hot tears flowed, indignant and sorrowful, the sanguine spirit of youth revived. "Sister Avice had told her how to be not loathly in the sight of those whom she could teach to love her."

There was one bound by a pledge! Ah, he would never fulfil it. If he should, Grisell felt a resolute purpose within her that though she could not be transformed, he should not see her loathly in his sight, and in that hope she slept.

Charlotte M. Yonge

CHAPTER IX

THE KING-MAKER

O where is faith? O where is loyalty?

SHAKESPEARE, Henry VI., Part II.

Grisell was disappointed in her hopes of seeing her Countess of Salisbury again, for as she rode into the Castle of York she heard the Earl's hearty voice of greeting. "Ha, stout Will of Whitburn, well met! What, from the north?"

The Earl stood talking with a tall brawny man, lean and strong, brown and weather-beaten, in a frayed suit of buff leather stained to all sorts of colours, in which rust predominated, and a face all brown and red except for the grizzled eyebrows, hair, and stubbly beard. She had not seen her father since she was five years old, and she would not have known him.

"I am from the south now, my lord," she heard his gruff voice say. "I have been taking my lad to be bred up in the Duke of York's house, for better nurture than can be had in my sea-side tower."

"Quite right. Well done in you," responded Warwick. "The Duke of York is the man to hold by. We have an exchange for you, a daughter for a son," and he was leading the way towards Grisell, who had just dismounted from her pony, and stood by it, trembling a little, and bending for her father's blessing. It was not more than a crossing of her, and he was talking all the time.

"Ha! how now! Methought my Lady of Salisbury had bestowed her in the Abbey - how call you it?"

"Aye," returned Warwick; "but since we have not had King or Parliament with spirit to stand up to the Pope, he thrusts his claw in everywhere, puts a strange Abbess into Wilton, and what must she do but send down her Proctor to treat the poor nunnery as it were a sponge, and spite of all my Lady Mother's bounties to the place, what lists he do but turn out the poor maid for lack of a dowry, not so much as giving time for a notice to be sent."

"If we had such a rogue in the North Country we should know how to serve him," observed Sir William, and Warwick laughed as befitted a Westmoreland Nevil, albeit he was used to more civilised ways.

"Scurvy usage," he said, "but the Prioress had no choice save to put her in such keeping as she could, and send her away to my Lady Mother, or failing her to her home."

"Soh! She must e'en jog off with me, though how it is to be with her my lady may tell, not I, since every groat those villain yeomen and fisher folk would raise, went to fit out young Rob, and there has not been so much as a Border raid these four years and more. There are the nuns at Gateshead, as hard as nails, will not hear of a maid without a dower, and yonder mansworn fellow Copeland casts her off like an old glove! Let us look at you, wench! Ha! Face is unsightly enough, but thou wilt not be a badly-made woman. Take heart, what's thy name - Grisell? May be there's luck for thee still, though it be hard of coming to Whitburn," he added, turning to Warwick. "There's this wench scorched to a cinder, enough to fright one, and my other lad racked from head to foot with pain and sores, so as it is a misery to hear the poor child cry out, and even if he be reared, he will be good for nought save a convent."

Grisell would fain have heard more about this poor little brother, but the ladies were entering the castle, and she had to follow them. She saw no more of her father except from the far end of the table, but orders were issued that she should be ready to accompany him on his homeward way the next morning at six o'clock. Her brother Robert had been sent in charge of some of the Duke of York's retainers, to join his household as a page, though they had missed him on the route, and the Lord of Whitburn was anxious to get home again, never being quite sure what the Scots, or the Percies, or his kinsmen of Gilsland, might attempt in his absence. "Though," as he said, "my lady was as good as a dozen men-at-arms, but somehow she had not been the same woman since little Bernard had fallen sick."

There was no one in the company with whom Grisell was very sorry to part, for though Dame Gresford had been kind to her, it had been merely the attending to the needs of a charge, not showing her any affection, and she had shrunk from the eyes of so large a party.

When she came down early into the hall, her father's half-dozen retainers were taking their morning meal at one end of a big board, while a manchet of bread and a silver cup of ale was ready for each of them at the other, and her father while swallowing his was in deep conversation over northern politics with the courteous Earl, who had come down to speed his guests. As she passed the retainers she heard, "Here comes our Grisly Grisell," and a smothered laugh, and in fact "Grisly Grisell" continued to be her name among the free-spoken people of the north. The Earl broke off, bowed to her, and saw that she was provided, breaking into his conversation with the Baron, evidently much to the impatience of the latter; and again the polite noble came down to the door with her, and placed her on her palfrey, bidding her a kind farewell ere she rode away with her father. It would be long before she met with such courtesy again. Her father called to his side his old, rugged-looking esquire Cuthbert Ridley, and began discussing with him what Lord Warwick had said, both wholly absorbed in the subject, and paying no attention to the girl who rode by the Baron's side, so that it was well that her old infantine training in horsemanship had come back to her.

She remembered Cuthbert Ridley, who had carried her about and petted her long ago, and, to her surprise, looked no older than he had done in those days when he had seemed to her infinitely aged. Indeed it was to him, far more than to her father, that she owed any attention or care taken of her on the journey. Her father was not unkind, but never seemed to recollect that she needed any more care than his rough followers, and once or twice he and all his people rode off headlong over the fell at sight of a stag roused by one of their great deer-hounds. Then Cuthbert Ridley kept beside her, and when the ground became too rough for a New Forest pony and a hand unaccustomed to northern ground, he drew up. She would probably - if not thrown and injured - have been left behind to feel herself lost on the moors. She minded the less his somewhat rude ejaculation, "Ho! Ho! South! South! Forgot how to back a horse on rough ground. Eh? And what a poor soft-paced beast! Only fit to ride on my lady's pilgrimage or in a State procession."

(He said Gang, but neither the Old English nor the northern dialect could be understood by the writer or the reader, and must be taken for granted.)

"They are all gone!" responded Grisell, rather frightened.

"Never guessed you were not among them," replied Ridley. "Why, my lady would be among the foremost, in at the death belike, if she did not cut the throat of the quarry."

Grisell could well believe it, but used to gentle nuns, she shuddered a little as she asked what they were to do next.

"Turn back to the track, and go softly on till my lord comes up with us," answered Ridley. "Or you might be fain to rest under a rock for a while."

The rest was far from unwelcome, and Grisell sat down on a mossy stone while Ridley gathered bracken for her shelter, and presently even brought her a branch or two of whortle-berries. She felt that she had a friend, and was pleased when he began to talk of how he remembered her long ago.

"Ah! I mind you, a little fat ball of a thing, when you were fetched home from Herring Dick's house, how you used to run after the dogs like a kitten after her tail, and used to crave to be put up on old Black Durham's back."

"I remember Black Durham! Had he not a white star on his forehead?"

"A white blaze sure enough."

"Is he at the tower still? I did not see him in the plump of spears."

"No, no, poor beast. He broke his leg four years ago come Martinmas, in a rabbit-hole on Berwick Law, last raid that we made, and I tarried to cut his throat with my dagger - though it went to my heart, for his good old eyes looked at me like Christians, and my lord told me I was a fool for my pains, for the Elliots were hard upon us, but I could not leave him to be a mark for them, and I was up with the rest in time, though I had to cut down the foremost lad."

Certainly "home" would be very unlike the experience of Grisell's education.

Ridley gave her a piece of advice. "Do not be daunted at my lady; her bark is ever worse than her bite, and what she will not bear with is the seeming cowed before her. She is all the sharper with her tongue now that her heart is sore for Master Bernard."

"What ails my brother Bernard?" then asked Grisell anxiously.

"The saints may know, but no man does, unless it was that Crooked Nan of Strait Glen overlooked the poor child," returned the esquire. "Ever since he fell into the red beck he hath done nought but peak and pine, and be twisted with cramps and aches, with sores breaking out on him; though there's a honeycomb-stone from Roker over his bed. My lord took out all the retainers to lay hold on Crooked Nan, but she got scent of it no doubt, for Jack of Burhill took his oath that he had seen a muckle hare run up the glen that morn, and when we got there she was not to be seen or heard of. We have heard of her in the Gilsland ground, where they would all the sooner see a the young lad of Whitburn crippled and a mere misery to see or hear."

Grisell was quite as ready to believe in witchcraft as was the old squire, and to tremble at their capacities for mischief. She asked what nunneries were near, and was disappointed to find nothing within easy reach. St. Cuthbert's diocese had not greatly favoured woman-kind, and Whitby was far away.

By and by her father came back, the thundering tramp of the horses being heard in time enough for her to spring up and be mounted again before he came in sight, the yeomen carrying the antlers and best portions of the deer.

"Left out, my wench," he shouted. "We must mount you better. Ho! Cuthbert, thou a squire of dames? Ha! Ha!"

"The maid could not be left to lose herself on the fells," muttered the squire, rather ashamed of his courtesy.

"She must get rid of nunnery breeding. We want no

trim and dainty lassies here," growled her father. "Look you, Ridley, that horse of Hob's -" and the rest was lost in a discussion on horseflesh.

Long rides, which almost exhausted Grisell, and halts in exceedingly uncomfortable hostels, where she could hardly obtain tolerable seclusion, brought her at last within reach of home. There was a tall church tower and some wretched hovels round it. The Lord of Whitburn halted, and blew his bugle with the peculiar note that signified his own return, then all rode down to the old peel, the outline of which Grisell saw with a sense of remembrance, against the gray sea-line, with the little breaking, glancing waves, which she now knew herself to have unconsciously wanted and missed for years past.

Whitburn Tower stood on the south side, on a steep cliff overlooking the sea. The peel tower itself looked high and strong, but to Grisell, accustomed to the widespread courts of the great castles and abbeys of the south, the circuit of outbuildings seemed very narrow and cramped, for truly there was need to have no more walls than could be helped for the few defenders to guard.

All was open now, and under the arched gateway, with the portcullis over her head, fitly framing her, stood the tall, gaunt figure of the lady, grayer, thinner, more haggard than when Grisell had last seen her, and beside her, leaning on a crutch, a white-faced boy, small and stunted for six years old.

"Ha, dame! Ha, Bernard; how goes it?" shouted the Baron in his gruff, hoarse voice.

"He willed to come down to greet you, though he cannot hold your stirrup," said the mother. "You are soon returned. Is all well with Rob?"

"O aye, I found Thorslan of Danby and a plump of spears on the way to the Duke of York at Windsor. They say he will need all his following if the Beauforts put it about that the King has recovered as much wit as ever he had. So I e'en sent Rob on with him, and came back so as to be ready in case there's a call for me. Soh! Berney; on thy feet again? That's well, my lad; but we'll have thee up the steps."

He seemed quite to have forgotten the presence of Grisell, and it was Cuthbert Ridley who helped her off her horse, but just then little Bernard in his father's arms exclaimed

"Black nun woman!"

"By St. Cuthbert!" cried the Baron, "I mind me! Here, wench! I have brought back the maid in her brother's stead."

And as Grisell, in obedience to his call, threw back her veil, Bernard screamed, "Ugsome wench, send her away!" threw his arms round his father's neck and hid his face with a babyish gesture.

"Saints have mercy!" cried the mother, "thou hast not mended much since I saw thee last. They that marred thee had best have kept thee. Whatever shall we do with the maid?"

"Send her away, the loathly thing," reiterated the boy, lifting up his head from his father's shoulder for another glimpse, which produced a puckering of the face in readiness for crying.

"Nay, nay, Bernard," said Ridley, feeling for the poor girl and speaking up for her when no one else would. "She is your sister, and you must be a fond brother to her, for an ill-nurtured lad spoilt her poor face when it was as fair as your own. Kiss your sister like a good lad, and -

"No! no!" shouted Bernard. "Take her away. I hate her." He began to cry and kick.

"Get out of his sight as fast as may be," commanded the mother, alarmed by her sickly darling's paroxysm of passion.

Grisell, scarce knowing where to go, could only allow herself to be led away by Ridley, who, seeing her tears, tried to comfort her in his rough way. "'Tis the petted bairn's way, you see, mistress - and my lady has no thought save for him. He will get over it soon enough when he learns your gentle convent-bred conditions."

Still the cry of "Grisly Griscll," picked up as if by instinct or by some echo from the rear of the escort, rang in her ears in the angry fretful voice of the poor little creature towards whom her heart was yearning. Even the two women-servants there were, no more looked at her askance, as they took her to a seat in the hall, and consulted where my lady would have her bestowed. She was wiping away bitter tears as she heard her only friend Cuthbert settle the matter. "The chamber within the solar is the place for the noble damsels."

"That is full of old armour, and dried herrings, and stockfish."

"Move them then! A fair greeting to give to my lord's daughter."

There was some further muttering about a bed, and Grisell sprang up. "Oh, hush! hush! I can sleep on a cloak; I have done so for many nights. Only let me be no burthen. Show me where I can go to be an anchoress, since they will not have me in a convent or anywhere," and bitterly she wept.

"Peace, peace, lady," said the squire kindly. "I will deal with these ill-tongued lasses. Shame on them! Go off, and make the chamber ready, or I'll find a scourge for you. And as to my lady - she is wrapped up in the sick bairn, but she has only to get used to you to be friendly enough."

"O what a hope in a mother," thought poor Grisell. "O that I were at Wilton or some nunnery, where my looks would be pardoned! Mother Avice, dear mother, what wouldst thou say to me now!"

The peel tower had been the original building, and was still as it were the citadel, but below had been built the very strong but narrow castle court, containing the stables and the well, and likewise the hall and kitchen - which were the dwelling and sleeping places of the men of the household, excepting Cuthbert Ridley, who being of gentle blood, would sit above the salt, and had his quarters with Rob when at home in the tower. The solar was a room above the hall, where was the great box-bed of the lord and lady, and a little bed for Bernard.

Entered through it, in a small turret, was a chamber designed for the daughters and maids, and this was rightly appropriated by Ridley to the Lady Grisell. The two women-servants - Bell and Madge - were wives to the cook and the castle smith, so the place had been disused and made a receptacle for drying fish, fruit, and the like. Thus the sudden call for its use provoked a storm of murmurs in no gentle voices, and Grisell shrank into a corner of the hall, only wishing she could efface herself.

And as she looked out on the sea from her narrow window, it seemed to her dismally gray, moaning, restless, and dreary.

CHAPTER X

COLD WELCOME

Seek not for others to love you,
But seek yourself to love them best,
And you shall find the secret true,
Of love and joy and rest.

I. WILLIAMS.

To lack beauty was a much more serious misfortune in the Middle Ages than at present. Of course it was probable that there might be a contract of marriage made entirely irrespective of attractiveness, long before the development of either of the principal parties concerned; but even then the rude, open-spoken husband would consider himself absolved from any attention to an ill-favoured wife, and the free tongues of her surroundings would not be slack to make her aware of her defects. The cloister was the refuge of the unmarried woman, if of gentle birth as a nun, if of a lower grade as a lay-sister; but the fifteenth century was an age neither of religion nor of chivalry. Dowers were more thought of than devotion in convents as elsewhere. Whitby being one of the oldest and grandest foundations was sure to be inaccessible to a high-born but unportioned girl, and Grisell in her sense of loneliness saw nothing before her but to become an anchoress, that is to say, a female hermit, such as generally lived in strict seclusion under shelter of the Church.

"There at least," thought poor Grisell, "there would be none to sting me to the heart with those jeering eyes of theirs. And I might feel in time that God and His Saints loved me, and not long for my father and mother, and oh! my poor little brother - yes, and Leonard Copeland, and Sister Avice, and the rest. But would Sister Avice call this devotion? Nay, would she not say that these cruel eyes and words are a cross upon me, and I must bear them and love in spite - at least till I be old enough to choose for myself?"

She was summoned to supper, and this increased the sense of dreariness, for Bernard screamed that the grisly one should not come near him, or he would not eat, and she had to take her meal of dried fish and barley bread in the wide chimney corner, where there always was a fire at every season of the year.

Her chamber, which Cuthbert Ridley's exertions had compelled the women to prepare for her, was - as seen in the light of the long evening - a desolate place, within a turret, opening from the solar, or chamber of her parents and Bernard, the loophole window devoid of glass, though a shutter could be closed in bad weather, the walls circular and of rough, untouched, unconcealed stone, a pallet bed - the only attempt at furniture, except one chest - and Grisell's own mails tumbled down anyhow, and all pervaded by an ancient and fishy smell. She felt too downhearted even to creep out and ask for a pitcher of water. She took a long look over the gray, heaving sea, and tired as she was, it was long before she could pray and cry herself to sleep, and accustomed as she was to convent beds, this one appeared to be stuffed with raw apples, and she awoke with aching bones.

Her request for a pitcher or pail of water was treated as southland finery, for those who washed at all used the horse trough, but fortunately for her Cuthbert Ridley heard the request. He had been enough in the south in attendance on his master to know how young damsels lived, and what treatment they met with, and he was soon rating the women in no measured terms for the disrespect they had presumed to show to the Lady Grisell, encouraged by the neglect of her parents

The Lord of Whitburn, appearing on the scene at the moment, backed up his retainer, and made it plain that he intended his daughter to be respected and obeyed, and the grumbling women had to submit. Nor did he refuse to acknowledge, on Ridley's representation, that Grisell ought to have an attendant of her own, and the lady of the castle, coming down with Bernard clinging to her skirt with one hand, and leaning on his crutch, consented. "If the maid was to be here, she must be treated fitly, and Bell and Madge had enough to do without convent-bred fancies."

So Cuthbert descended the steep path to the ravine where dwelt the fisher folk, and came back with a girl barefooted, bareheaded, with long, streaming, lint-white locks, and the scantiest of garments, crying bitterly with fright, and almost struggling to go back. She was the orphan remnant of a family drowned in the bay, and was a burthen on her fisher kindred, who were rejoiced thus to dispose of her.

She sobbed the more at sight of the grisly lady, and

almost screamed when Grisell smiled and tried to take her by the hand. Ridley fairly drove her upstairs, step by step, and then shut her in with his young lady, when she sank on the floor and hid her face under all her bleached hair.

"Poor little thing," thought Grisell; "it is like having a fresh-caught sea-gull. She is as forlorn as I am, and more afraid!"

So she began to speak gently and coaxingly, begging the girl to look up, and assuring her that she would not be hurt. Grisell had a very soft and persuasive voice. Her chief misfortune as regarded her appearance was that the muscles of one cheek had been so drawn that though she smiled sweetly with one side of her face, the other was contracted and went awry, so that when the kind tones had made the girl look up for a moment, the next she cried, "O don't - don't! Holy Mary, forbid the spell!"

"I have no spells, my poor maid; indeed I am only a poor girl, a stranger here in my own home. Come, and do not fear me."

"Madge said you had witches' marks on your face," sobbed the child.

"Only the marks of gunpowder," said Grisell. "Listen, I will tell thee what befell me."

Gunpowder seemed to be quite beyond all experience of Whitburn nature, but the history of the catastrophe gained attention, and the girl's terror abated, so that Grisell could ask her name, which was Thora, and learning, too, that she had led a hard life since her granny died, and her uncle's wife beat her, and made her carry heavy loads of seaweed when it froze her hands, besides a hundred other troubles. As to knowing any kind of feminine art, she was as ignorant as if the rough and extremely dirty woollen garment she wore, belted round with a strip of leather, had grown upon her, and though Grisell's own stock of garments was not extensive, she was obliged, for very shame, to dress this strange attendant in what she could best spare, as well as, in spite of sobs and screams, to wash her face, hands, and feet, and it was wonderful how great a difference this made in the wild creature by the time the clang of the castle bell summoned all to the midday meal, when as before, Bernard professed not to be able to look at his sister, but when she had retreated he was seen spying at her through his fingers, with great curiosity.

Afterwards she went up to her mother to beg for a few necessaries for herself and for her maid, and to offer to do some spinning. She was not very graciously answered; but she was allowed an old frayed horse-cloth on which Thora might sleep, and for the rest she might see what she could find under the stairs in the turret, or in the chest in the hall window.

The broken, dilapidated fragments which seemed to Grisell mere rubbish were treasures and wonders to Thora, and out of them she picked enough to render her dreary chamber a very few degrees more habitable. Thora would sleep there, and certainly their relations were reversed, for carrying water was almost the only office she performed at first, since Grisell had to dress her, and teach her to keep herself in a tolerable state of neatness, and likewise how to spin, luring her with the hope of spinning yarn for a new dress for herself. As to prayers, her mind was a mere blank, though she said something that sounded like a spell except that it began with "Pater." She did not know who made her, and entirely believed in Niord and Rana, the storm-gods of Norseland. Yet she had always been to mass every Sunday morning. So went all the family at the castle as a matter of course, but except when the sacring-bell hushed them, the Baron freely discussed crops or fish with the tenants, and the lady wrangled about dues of lambs, eggs, and fish. Grisell's attention was a new thing, and the priest's pronunciation was so defective to her ear that she could hardly follow.

That first week Grisell had plenty of occupation in settling her room and training her uncouth maid, who proved a much more apt scholar than she had expected, and became devoted to her like a little faithful dog.

No one else took much notice of either, except that at times Cuthbert Ridley showed himself to be willing to stand up for her. Her father was out a great deal, hunting or hawking or holding consultations with neighbouring knights or the men of Sunderland. Her mother, with the loudest and most peremptory of voices, ruled over the castle, ordered the men on their guards and at the stables, and the cook, scullions, and other servants, but without much good effect as household affairs were concerned, for the meals were as far removed from the delicate, dainty serving of the simplest fast-day meal at Wilton as from the sumptuous plenty and variety of Warwick house, and Bernard often cried and could not eat. She longed to make up for him one of the many appetising possets well known at Wilton, but her mother and Ralf the cook both scouted her first proposal. They wanted no south-bred meddlers over their fire.

However, one evening when Bernard had been fretful and in pain, the Baron had growled out that the child was cockered beyond all bearing, and the mother had flown out at the unnatural father, and on his half laughing at her doting ways, had actually rushed across with clenched fist to box his ears; he had muttered that the pining brat and shrewish dame made the house no place for him, and wandered out to the society of his horses. Lady Whitburn, after exhaling her wrath in abuse of him and all around, carried the child up to his bed. There he was moaning, and she trying to soothe him, when, darkness having put a stop to Grisell's spinning, she went to her chamber with Thora. In passing, the moaning was still heard, and she even thought her mother was crying. She ventured to approach and ask, "Fares he no better? If I might rub that poor leg."

But Bernard peevishly hid his face and whined, "Go away, Grisly," and her mother exclaimed, "Away with you, I have enough to vex me here without you."

She could only retire as fast as possible, and her tears ran down her face as in the long summer twilight she recited the evening offices, the same in which Sister Avice was joining in Wilton chapel. Before they were over she heard her father come up to bed, and in a harsh and angered voice bid Bernard to be still. There was stillness for some little time, but by and by the moaning and sobbing began again, and there was a jangling between the gruff voice and the shrill one, now thinner and weaker. Grisell felt that she must try again, and crept out. "If I might rub him a little while, and you rest, Lady Mother. He cannot see me now."

She prevailed , or rather the poor mother's utter

weariness and dejection did, together with the father's growl, "Let her bring us peace if she can."

Lady Whitburn let her kneel down by the bed, and guided her hand to the aching thigh.

"Soft! Soft! Good! Good!" muttered Bernard presently. "Go on!"

Grisell had acquired something of that strange almost magical touch of Sister Avice, and Bernard lay still under her hand. Her mother, who was quite worn out, moved to her own bed, and fell asleep, while the snores of the Baron proclaimed him to have been long appeased. The boy, too, presently was breathing softly, and Grisell's attitude relaxed, as her prayers and her dreams mingled together, and by and by, what she thought was the organ in Wilton chapel, and the light of St. Edith's taper, proved to be the musical rush of the incoming tide, and the golden sunrise over the sea, while all lay sound asleep around her, and she ventured gently to withdraw into her own room.

That night was Grisell's victory, though Bernard still held aloof from her all the ensuing day, when he was really the better and fresher for his long sleep, but at bed-time, when as usual the pain came on, he wailed for her to rub him, and as it was still daylight, and her father had gone out in one of the boats to fish, she ventured on singing to him, as she rubbed, to his great delight and still greater boon to her yearning heart. Even by day, as she sat at work, the little fellow limped up to her, and said, "Grisly, sing that again," staring hard in her face as she did so.

Charlotte M. Yonge

CHAPTER XI

BERNARD

I do remember an apothecary, -
And hereabouts he dwells.

SHAKESPEARE, Romeo and Juliet.

Bernard's affection was as strong as his aversion had been. Poor little boy, no one had been accustomed enough to sickly children, or indeed to children at all, to know how to make him happy or even comfortable, and his life had been sad and suffering ever since the blight that had fallen on him, through either the evil eye of Nan the witch, or through his fall into a freezing stream. His brother, a great strong lad, had teased and bullied him; his father, though not actually unkind except when wearied by his fretfulness, held him as a miserable failure, scarcely worth rearing; his mother, though her pride was in her elder son, and the only softness in her heart for the little one, had been so rugged and violent a woman all the years of her life, and had so despised all gentler habits of civilisation, that she really did not know how to be tender to the child who was really her darling. Her infants had been nursed in the cottages, and not returned to the castle till they were old enough to rough it - indeed they were soon sent off to be bred up elsewhere. Some failure in health, too, made it harder for her to be patient with an ailing child, and her love was apt to take the form of anger with his petulance or even with his suffering, or else of fierce battles with her husband in his defence.

The comfort would have been in burning Crooked Nan, but that beldame had disposed of herself out of reach, though Lady Whitburn still cherished the hope of forcing the Gilsland Dacres or the Percies to yield the woman up. Failing this, the boy had been shown to a travelling friar, who had promised cure through the relics he carried about; but Bernard had only screamed at him, and had been none the better.

And now the little fellow had got over the first shock, he found that "Grisly," as he still called her, but only as an affectionate abbreviation, was the only person who could relieve his pain, or amuse him, in the whole castle; and he was incessantly hanging on her. She must put him to bed and sing lullabies to him, she must rub his limbs when they ached with rheumatic pains; hers was the only hand which might touch the sores that continually broke out, and he would sit for long spaces on her lap, sometimes stroking down the scar and pitying it with "Poor Grisly; when I am a man, I will throw down my glove, and fight with that lad, and kill him."

"O nay, nay, Bernard; he never meant to do me evil. He is a fair, brave, good boy."

"He scorned and ran away from you. He is mansworn and recreant," persisted Bernard. "Rob and I will make him say that you are the fairest of ladies."

"O nay, nay. That he could not."

"But you are, you are - on this side - mine own Grisly," cried Bernard, whose experiences of fair ladies had not been extensive, and who curled himself on her lap, giving unspeakable rest and joy to her weary, yearning spirit, as she pressed him to her breast. "Now, a story, a story," he entreated, and she was rich in tales from Scripture history and legends of the Saints, or she would sing her sweet monastic hymns and chants, as he nestled in her lap.

The mother had fits of jealousy at the exclusive preference, and now and then would rail at Grisell for cosseting the bairn and keeping him a helpless baby; or at Bernard for leaving his mother for this ill-favoured, useless sister, and would even snatch away the boy, and declare that she wanted no one to deal with him save herself; but Bernard had a will of his own, and screamed for his Grisly, throwing himself about in such a manner that Lady Whitburn was forced to submit, and quite to the alarm of her daughter, on one of these occasions she actually burst into a flood of tears, sobbing loud and without restraint. Indeed, though she hotly declared that she ailed nothing, there was a lassitude about her that made it a relief to have the care of Bernard taken off her hands; and the Baron's grumbling at disturbed nights made the removal of Bernard's bed to his sister's room generally acceptable.

Once, when Grisell was found to have taught both him and Thora the English version of the Lord's Prayer and Creed, and moreover to be telling him the story of the Gospel, there came, no one knew from where, an accusation which made her father tramp up and say, "Mark you, wench, I'll have no Lollards here."

"Lollards, sir; I never saw a Lollard!" said Grisell trembling.

"Where, then, didst learn all this, making holy things common?"

"We all learnt it at Wilton, sir, from the reverend mothers and the holy father."

The Baron was fairly satisfied, and muttered that if the bairn was fit only for a shaveling, it might be all right.

Poor child, would he ever be fit for that or any occupation of manhood? However, Grisell had won permission to compound broths, cakes, and possets for him, over the hall fire, for the cook and his wife would not endure her approach to their domain, and with great reluctance allowed her the materials. Bernard watched her operations with intense delight and amusement, and tasted with a sense of triumph and appetite, calling on his mother to taste likewise; and she, on whose palate semi-raw or over-roasted joints had begun to pall, allowed that the nuns had taught Grisell something.

And thus as time went on Grisell led no unhappy life. Every one around was used to her scars, and took no notice of them, and there was nothing to bring the thought before her, except now and then when a fishwife's baby, brought to her for cure, would scream at her. She never went beyond the castle except to mass, now and then to visit a sick person, and to seek some of the herbs of which she had learnt the use, and then she was always attended by Thora and Ridley, who made a great favour of going.

Charlotte M. Yonge

Bernard had given her the greater part of his heart, and she soothed his pain, made his hours happy, and taught him the knowledge she brought from the convent. Her affections were with him, and though her mother could scarcely be said to love her, she tolerated and depended more and more on the daughter who alone could give her more help or solace.

That was Grisell's second victory, when she was actually asked to compound a warm, relishing, hot bowl for her father when be was caught in a storm and came in drenched and weary.

She wanted to try on her little brother the effect of one of Sister Avice's ointments, which she thought more likely to be efficacious than melted mutton fat, mixed with pounded worms, scrapings from the church bells, and boiled seaweed, but some of her ingredients were out of reach, unless they were attainable at Sunderland, and she obtained permission to ride thither under the escort of Cuthbert Ridley, and was provided with a small purse - the proceeds of the Baron's dues out of the fishermen's sales of herrings.

She was also to purchase a warm gown and mantle for her mother, and enough of cloth to afford winter garments for Bernard; and a steady old pack-horse carried the bundles of yarn to be exchanged for these commodities, since the Whitburn household possessed no member dexterous with the old disused loom, and the itinerant weavers did not come that way - it was whispered because they were afraid of the fisher folk, and got but sorry cheer from the lady.

The commissions were important, and Grisell enjoyed the two miles' ride along the cliffs of Roker Bay, looking up at the curious caverns in the rock, and seeking for the very strangely-formed stones supposed to have magic power, which fell from the rock. In the distance beyond the river to the southward, Ridley pointed to the tall square tower of Monks Wearmouth Church dominating the great monastery around it, which had once held the venerable Bede, though to both Ridley and Grisell he was only a name of a patron saint.

The harbour formed by the mouth of the river Wear was a marvel to Grisell, crowded as it was with low, squarely-rigged and gaily-coloured vessels of Holland, Friesland, and Flanders, very new sights to one best acquainted with Noah's ark or St. Peter's ship in illuminations.

"Sunderland is a noted place for shipbuilding," said Ridley. "Moreover, these come for wool, salt-fish, and our earth coal, and they bring us fine cloth, linen, and stout armour. I am glad to see yonder Flemish ensign. If luck goes well with us, I shall get a fresh pair of gauntlets for my lord, straight from Gaunt, the place of gloves."

"GANT for glove," said Grisell.

"How? You speak French. Then you may aid me in chaffering, and I will straight to the Fleming, with whom I may do better than with Hodge of the Lamb. How now, here's a shower coming up fast!"

It was so indeed; a heavy cloud had risen quickly, and was already bursting overhead. Ridley hurried on, along a thoroughfare across salt marshes (nowdocks), but the speed was not enough to prevent their being drenched by a torrent of rain and hail before they reached the tall-timbered houses of Wearmouth.

"In good time!" cried Ridley; "here's the Poticary's sign! You had best halt here at once."

In front of a high-roofed house with a projecting upper story, hung a sign bearing a green serpent on a red ground, over a stall, open to the street, which the owner was sheltering with a deep canvas awning.

"Hola, Master Lambert Groats," called Ridley. "Here's the young demoiselle of Whitburn would have some dealings with you."

Jumping off his horse, he helped Grisell to dismount just as a small, keen-faced, elderly man in dark gown came forward, doffing his green velvet cap, and hoping the young lady would take shelter in his poor house.

Grisell, glancing round the little booth, was aware of sundry marvellous curiosities hanging round, such as a dried crocodile, the shells of tortoises, of sea-urchins and crabs, all to her eyes most strange and weird; but Master Lambert was begging her to hasten in at once to his dwelling-room beyond, and let his wife dry her clothes, and at once there came forward a plump, smooth, pleasant-looking personage, greatly his junior, dressed in a tight gold-edged cap over her fair hair, a dark skirt, black bodice, bright apron, and white sleeves, curtseying low, but making signs to invite the newcomers to the fire on the hearth. "My housewife is stone deaf," explained their host, "and she knows no tongue save her own, and the unspoken language of courtesy, but she is rejoiced to welcome the demoiselle. Ah, she is drenched! Ah, if she will honour my poor house!"

The wife curtsied low, and by hospitable signs prayed the demoiselle to come to the fire, and take off her wet mantle. It was a very comfortable room, with a wide chimney, and deep windows glazed with thick circles of glass, the spaces between leaded around in diamond panes, through which vine branches could dimly be seen flapping and beating in the storm. A table stood under one with various glasses and vessels of curious shapes, and a big book, and at the other was a distaff, a work-basket, and other feminine gear. Shelves with pewter dishes, and red, yellow, and striped crocks, surrounded the walls; there was a savoury cauldron on the open fire. It was evidently sitting-room and kitchen in one, with offices beyond, and Grisell was at once installed in a fine carved chair by the fire - a more comfortable seat than had ever fallen to her share.

"Look you here, mistress," said Ridley; "you are in safe quarters here, and I will leave you awhile, take the horses to the hostel, and do mine errands across the river - 'tis not fit for you - and come back to you when the shower is over, and you can come and chaffer for your woman's gear."

From the two good hosts the welcome was decided, and Grisell was glad to have time for consultation. An Apothecary of those days did not rise to the dignity of a leech, but was more like the present owner of a chemist's shop, though a chemist then meant something much more abstruse, who studied occult sciences, such as alchemy and astrology.

In fact, Lambert Groot, which was his real name, though English lips had made it Groats, belonged to one of the prosperous guilds of the great merchant city of Bruges, but he had offended his family by his determination to marry the deaf, and almost dumb, portionless orphan daughter of an old friend and contemporary, and to save her from the scorn and slights of his relatives - though she was quite as well-born as themselves - he had migrated to England, where Wearmouth and Sunderland had a brisk trade with the Low Countries. These cities enjoyed the cultivation of the period, and this room, daintily clean and fresh, seemed to Grisell more luxurious than any she had seen since the Countess of Warwick's. A silver bowl of warm soup, extracted from the pot au feu, was served to her by the Hausfrau, on a little table, spread with a fine white cloth edged with embroidery, with an earnest gesture begging her to partake, and a slender Venice glass of wine was brought to her with a cake of wheaten bread. Much did Grisell wish she could have transferred such refreshing fare to Bernard. She ventured to ask "Master Poticary" whether he sold "Balsam of Egypt." He was interested at once, and asked whether it were for her own use.

"Nay, good master, you are thinking of my face; but that was a burn long ago healed. It is for my poor little brother."

Therewith Grisell and Master Groats entered on a discussions of symptoms, drugs, ointments, and ingredients, in which she learnt a good deal and perhaps disclosed more of Sister Avice's methods than Wilton might have approved. In the midst the sun broke out gaily after the shower, and disclosed, beyond the window, a garden where every leaf and spray were glittering and glorious with their own diamond drops in the sunshine. A garden of herbs was a needful part of an apothecary's business, as he manufactured for himself all of the medicaments which he did not import from foreign parts, but this had been laid out between its high walls with all the care, taste, and precision of the Netherlander, and Grisell exclaimed in perfect ecstasy: "Oh, the garden, the garden! I have seen nothing so fair and sweet since I left Wilton."

Master Lambert was delighted, and led her out. There is no describing how refreshing was the sight to eyes after the bare, dry walls of the castle, and the tossing sea which the maiden had not yet learnt to love. Nor was the garden dull, though meant for use. There was a well in the centre with roses trained over it, roses of the dark old damask kind and the dainty musk, used to be distilled for the eyes, some flowers lingering still; there was the brown dittany or fraxinella, whose dried blossoms are phosphoric at night; delicate pink centaury, good for ague; purple mallows, good for wounds; leopard's bane with yellow blossoms; many and many more old and dear friends of Grisell, redolent of Wilton cloister and Sister Avice; and she ran from one to the other quite transported, and forgetful of all the dignities of the young Lady of Whitburn, while Lambert was delighted, and hoped she would come again when his lilies were in bloom.

So went the time till Ridley returned, and when the price was asked of the packet of medicaments prepared for her, Lambert answered that the value was fully balanced by what he had learnt from the lady. This, however, did not suit the honour of the Dacres, and Grisell, as well as her squire, who looked offended, insisted on leaving two gold crowns in payment. The Vrow kissed her hand, putting into it the last sprays of roses, which Grisell cherished in her bosom.

She was then conducted to a booth kept by a Dutchman, where she obtained the warm winter garments that she needed for her mother and brother, and likewise some linen, for the Lady of Whitburn had never been housewife enough to keep up a sufficient supply for Bernard, and Grisell was convinced that the cleanliness which the nuns had taught her would mitigate his troubles. With Thora to wash for her she hoped to institute a new order of things.

Much pleased with her achievements she rode home. She was met there by more grumbling than satisfaction. Her father had expected more coin to send to Robert, who, like other absent youths, called for supplies.

The yeoman who had gone with him returned, bearing a scrap of paper with the words:-

"MINE HONOURED LORD AND FATHER - I pray you to send me Black Lightning and xvj crowns by the hand of Ralf, and so the Saints have you in their keeping. - Your dutiful sonne,

"ROBERT DACRE."

xvj crowns were a heavy sum in those days, and Lord Whitburn vowed that he had never so called on his father except when he was knighted, but those were the good old days when spoil was to be won in France. What could Rob want of such a sum?

"Well-a-day, sir, the house of the Duke of York is no place to stint in. The two young Earls of March and of Rutland, as they call them, walk in red and blue and gold bravery, and chains of jewels, even like king's sons, and none of the squires and pages can be behind them."

"Black Lightning too, my best colt, when I deemed the lad fitted out for years to come. I never sent home the like message to my father under the last good King Henry, but purveyed myself of a horse on the battlefield more than once. But those good old days are over, and lads think more of velvet and broidery than of lances and swords. Forsooth, their coats-of-arms are good to wear on silk robes instead of helm and shield; and as to our maids, give them their rein, and they spend more than all the rest on women's tawdry gear!"

Poor Grisell! when she had bought nothing ornamental, and nothing for herself except a few needles.

However, in spite of murmurs, the xvj crowns were raised and sent away with Black Lightning; and as time went on Grisell became more and more a needful person. Bernard was stronger, and even rode out on a pony, and the fame of his improvement brought other patients to the Lady Grisell from the vassals, with whom she dealt as best she might, successfully or the reverse, while her mother, as her health failed, let fall more and more the reins of household rule.

Charlotte M. Yonge

CHAPTER XII

WORD FROM THE WARS

Above, below, the Rose of Snow,
Twined with her blushing face we spread.

GRAY'S Bard.

News did not travel very fast to Whitburn, but one summer's day a tall, gallant, fair-faced esquire, in full armour of the cumbrous plate fashion, rode up to the gate, and blew the family note on his bugle.

"My son! my son Rob," cried the lady, starting up from the cushions with which Grisell had furnished her settle.

Robert it was, who came clanking in, met by his father at the gate, by his mother at the door, and by Bernard on his crutch in the rear, while Grisell, who had never seen this brother, hung back.

The youth bent his knee, but his outward courtesy did not conceal a good deal of contempt for the rude northern habits. "How small and dark the hall is! My lady, how old you have grown! What, Bernard, still fit only for a shaven friar! Not shorn yet, eh? Ha! is that Grisell? St. Cuthbert to wit! Copeland has made a hag of her!"

"'Tis a good maid none the less," replied her father; the first direct praise that she had ever had from him, and which made her heart glow.

"She will ne'er get a husband, with such a visage as that," observed Robert, who did not seem to have learnt courtesy or forbearance yet on his travels; but he was soon telling his father what concerned them far more than the maiden's fate.

"Sir, I have come on the part of the Duke of York to summon you. What, you have not heard? He needs, as speedily as may be, the arms of every honest man. How many can you get together?"

"But what is it? How is it? Your Duke ruled the roast last time I heard of him."

"You know as little as my horse here in the north!" cried Rob.

"This I did hear last time there was a boat come in, that the Queen, that mother of mischief, had tried to lay hands on our Lord of Salisbury, and that he and your Duke of York had soundly beaten her and the men of Cheshire."

"Yea, at Blore Heath; and I thought to win my spurs on the Copeland banner, but even as I was making my way to it and the recreant that bore it, I was stricken across my steel cap and dazed."

"I'll warrant it," muttered his father.

"When I could look up again all was changed, the banner nowhere in sight, but I kept my saddle, and cut down half a dozen rascaille after that."

"Ha!" half incredulously, for it was a mere boy who boasted. "That's my brave lad! And what then? More hopes of the spurs, eh?"

"Then what does the Queen do, but seeing that no one would willingly stir a lance against an old witless saint like King Harry, she gets a host together, dragging the poor man hither and thither with her, at Ludlow. Nay, we even heard the King was dead, and a mass was said for the repose of his soul, but with the morning what should we see on the other side of the river Teme but the royal standard, and who should be under it but King Harry himself with his meek face and fair locks, twirling his fingers after his wont. So the men would have it that they had been gulled, and they fell away one after another, till there was nothing for it but for the Duke and his sons, and my Lords of Salisbury and Warwick and a few score more of us, to ride off as best we might, with Sir Andrew Trollope and his men after us, as hard as might be, so that we had to break up, and keep few together. I went with the Duke of York and young Lord Edmund into Wales, and thence in a bit of a fishing-boat across to Ireland. Ask me to fight in full field with twice the numbers, but never ask me to put to sea again! There's nothing like it for taking heart and soul out of a man!"

"I have crossed the sea often enow in the good old days, and known nothing worse than a qualm or two."

"That was to France," said his son. "This Irish Sea is far wider and far more tossing, I know for my own part. I'd have given a knight's fee to any one who would have thrown me overboard. I felt like an empty bag! But once there, they could not make enough of us. The Duke had got their hearts before, and odd sort of hearts they are. I was deaf with the wild kernes shouting round about in their gibberish - such figures, too, as they are, with their blue cloaks, streaming hair, and long glibbes (moustaches), and the Lords of the Pale, as they call the English sort, are nigh about as wild and savage as the mere Irish. It was as much as my Lord Duke could do to hinder two of them from coming to blows in his presence; and you should have heard them howl at one another. However, they are all with him, and a mighty force of them mean to go back with him to England. My Lord of Warwick came from Calais to hold counsel with him, and they have sworn to one another to meet with all their forces, and require the removal of the King's evil councillors; and my Lord Duke, with his own mouth, bade me go and summon his trusty Will Dacre of Whitburn - so he spake, sir - to be with him with all the spears and bowmen you can raise or call for among the neighbours. And it is my belief, sir, that he means not to stop at the councillors, but to put forth his rights. Hurrah for King Richard of the White Rose!" ended Robert, throwing up his cap.

"Nay, now," said his father. "I'd be loth to put down our gallant King Harry's only son."

"No one breathes a word against King Harry," returned Robert, "no more than against a carven saint in a church, and he is about as much of a king as old stone King Edmund, or King Oswald, or whoever he is, over the porch. He is welcome to reign as long as he likes or lives, provided he lets our Duke govern for him, and rids the country of the foreign woman and her brat, who is no more hers than I am, but a mere babe of Westminster town carried into the palace when the poor King Harry was beside himself."

"Nay, now, Rob!" cried his mother.

"So 'tis said!" sturdily persisted Rob. "'Tis well known that the King never looked at him the first time he was shown the little imp, and next time, when he was not so distraught, he lifted up his hands and said he wotted nought of the matter. Hap what hap, King Harry may roam from Church to shrine, from Abbey to chantry, so long as he lists, but none of us will brook to be ruled or misruled by the foreign woman and the Beauforts in his name, nor reigned over by the French dame or the beggar's brat, and the traitor coward Beaufort, but be under our own noble Duke and the White Rose, the only badge that makes the Frenchman flee."

The boy was scarcely fifteen, but his political tone, as of one who knew the world, made his father laugh and say, "Hark to the cockerel crowing loud. Spurs forsooth!"

"The Lords Edward and Edmund are knighted," grunted Rob, "and there's but few years betwixt us."

"But a good many earldoms and lands," said the Baron. "Hadst spoken of being out of pagedom, 'twere another thing."

"You are coming, sir," cried Rob, willing to put by the subject. "You are coming to see how I can win honours."

"Aye, aye," said his father. "When Nevil calls, then must Dacre come, though his old bones might well be at rest now. Salisbury and Warwick taking to flight like attainted traitors to please the foreign woman, saidst thou? Then it is the time men were in the saddle."

"Well I knew you would say so, and so I told my lord," exclaimed Robert.

"Thou didst, quotha? Without doubt the Duke was greatly reassured by thy testimony," said his father drily, while the mother, full of pride and exultation in her goodly firstborn son, could not but exclaim, "Daunt him not, my lord; he has done well thus to be sent home in charge."

"*I* daunt him?" returned Lord Whitburn, in his teasing mood. "By his own showing not a troop of Somerset's best horsemen could do that!"

Therewith more amicably, father and son fell to calculations of resources, which they kept up all through supper-time, and all the evening, till the names of Hobs, Wills, Dicks, and the like rang like a repeating echo in Grisell's ears. All through those long days of summer the father and son were out incessantly, riding from one tenant or neighbour to another, trying to raise men-at-arms and means to equip them if raised. All the dues on the herring-boats and the two whalers, on which Grisell had reckoned for the winter needs, were pledged to Sunderland merchants for armour and weapons; the colts running wild on the moors were hastily caught, and reduced to a kind of order by rough breaking in. The women of the castle and others requisitioned from the village toiled under the superintendence of the lady and Grisell at preparing such provision and equipments as were portable, such as dried fish, salted meat, and barley cakes, as well as linen, and there was a good deal of tailoring of a rough sort at jerkins, buff coats, and sword belts, not by any means the gentle work of embroidering pennons or scarves notable in romance.

"Besides," scoffed Robert, "who would wear Grisly Grisell's scarf!"

"I would," manfully shouted Bernard; "I would cram it down the throat of that recreant Copeland."

"Oh! hush, hush, Bernard," exclaimed Grisell, who was toiling with aching fingers at the repairs of her father's greasy old buff coat. "Such things are, as Robin well says, for noble demoiselles with fair faces and leisure times like the Lady Margaret. And oh, Robin, you have never told me of the Lady Margaret, my dear mate at Amesbury."

"What should I know of your Lady Margarets and such gear," growled Robin, whose chivalry had not reached the point of caring for ladies.

"The Lady Margaret Plantagenet, the young Lady Margaret of York," Grisell explained.

"Oh! That's what you mean is it? There's a whole troop of wenches at the high table in hall. They came after us with the Duchess as soon as we were settled in Trim Castle, but they are kept as demure and mim as may be in my lady's bower; and there's a pretty sharp eye kept on them. Some of the young squires who are fools enough to hanker after a few maids or look at the fairer ones get their noses wellnigh pinched off by Proud Cis's Mother of the Maids."

"Then it would not avail to send poor Grisell's greetings by you."

"I should like to see myself delivering them! Besides, we shall meet my lord in camp, with no cumbrance of woman gear."

Lord Whitburn's own castle was somewhat of a perplexity to him, for though his lady had once been quite sufficient captain for his scanty garrison, she was in too uncertain health, and what was worse, too much broken in spirit and courage, to be fit for the charge. He therefore decided on leaving Cuthbert Ridley, who, in winter at least, was scarcely as capable of roughing it as of old, to protect the castle, with a few old or partly disabled men, who could man the walls to some degree, therefore it was unlikely that there would be any attack.

So on a May morning the old, weather-beaten Dacre pennon with its three crusading scallop-shells, was uplifted in the court, and round it mustered about thirty men, of whom eighteen had been raised by the baron, some being his own vassals, and others hired at Sunderland. The rest were volunteers - gentlemen, their younger sons, and their attendants - placing themselves under his leadership, either from goodwill to York and Nevil, or from love of enterprise and hope of plunder.

CHAPTER XIII

A KNOT

I would mine heart had caught that wound
And slept beside him rather!
I think it were a better thing
Than murdered friend and marriage-ring
Forced on my life together.

E. B. BROWNING, The Romaunt of the Page.

Ladies were accustomed to live for weeks, months, nay, years, without news of those whom they had sent to the wars, and to live their life without them. The Lady of Whitburn did not expect to see her husband or son again till the summer campaign was over, and she was not at all uneasy about them, for the full armour of a gentleman had arrived at such a pitch of perfection that it was exceedingly difficult to kill him, and such was the weight, that his danger in being overthrown was of never being able to get up, but lying there to be smothered, made prisoner, or killed, by breaking into his armour. The knights could not have moved at all under the weight if they had not been trained from infancy, and had nearly reduced themselves to the condition of great tortoises.

It was no small surprise when, very late on a July

evening, when, though twilight still prevailed, all save the warder were in bed, and he was asleep on his post, a bugle-horn rang out the master's note, at first in the usual tones, then more loudly and impatiently. Hastening out of bed to her loophole window, Grisell saw a party beneath the walls, her father's scallop-shells dimly seen above them, and a little in the rear, one who was evidently a prisoner.

The blasts grew fiercer, the warder and the castle were beginning to be astir, and when Grisell hurried into the outer room, she found her mother afoot and hastily dressing.

"My lord! my lord! it is his note," she cried.

"Father come home!" shouted Bernard, just awake. "Grisly! Grisly! help me don my clothes."

Lady Whitburn trembled and shook with haste, and Grisell could not help her very rapidly in the dark, with Bernard howling rather than calling for help all the time; and before she, still less Grisell, was fit for the public, her father's heavy step was on the stairs, and she heard fragments of his words.

"All abed! We must have supper - ridden from Ayton since last baiting. Aye, got a prisoner - young Copeland - old one slain - great victory - Northampton. King taken - Buckingham and Egremont killed - Rob well - proud as a pyet. Ho, Grisell," as she appeared, "bestir thyself. We be ready to eat a horse behind the saddle. Serve up as fast as may be."

Grisell durst not stop to ask whether she had heard the word Copeland aright, and ran downstairs with a throbbing heart, just crossing the hall, where she thought she saw a figure bowed down, with hands over his face and elbows on his knees, but she could not pause, and went on to the kitchen, where the peat fire was never allowed to expire, and it was easy to stir it into heat. Whatever was cold she handed over to the servants to appease the hunger of the arrivals, while she broiled steaks, and heated the great perennial cauldron of broth with all the expedition in her power, with the help of Thora and the grumbling cook, when he appeared, angry at being disturbed.

Morning light was beginning to break before her toils were over for the dozen hungry men pounced so suddenly in on her, and when she again crossed the hall, most of them were lying on the straw-bestrewn floor fast asleep. One she specially noticed, his long limbs stretched out as he lay on his side, his head on his arm, as if he had fallen asleep from extreme fatigue in spite of himself.

His light brown hair was short and curly, his cheeks fair and ruddy, and all reminded her of Leonard Copeland as he had been those long years ago before her accident. Save for that, she would have been long ago his wife, she with her marred face the mate of that nobly fair countenance. How strange to remember. How she would have loved him, frank and often kind as she remembered him, though rough and impatient of restraint. What was that which his fingers had held till sleep had unclasped them? An ivory chessrook! Such was a favourite token of ladies to their true loves. What did it mean? Might she pause to pray a prayer over him as once hers - that all might be well with him, for she knew that in this unhappy war important captives were not treated as Frenchmen would have been as prisoners of war, but executed as traitors to their King.

She paused over him till a low sound and the bright eyes of one of the dogs warned her that all might in another moment be awake, and she fled up the stair to the solar, where her parents were both fast asleep, and across to her own room, where she threw herself on her bed, dressed as she was, but could not sleep for the multitude of strange thoughts that crowded over her in the increasing daylight.

By and by there was a stir, some words passed in the outer room, and then her mother came in.

"Wake, Grisly. Busk and bonne for thy wedding-morning instantly. Copeland is to keep his troth to thee at once. The Earl of Warwick hath granted his life to thy father on that condition only."

"Oh, mother, is he willing?" cried Grisell trembling.

"What skills that, child? His hand was pledged, and he must fulfil his promise now that we have him."

"Was it troth? I cannot remember it," said Grisell.

"That matters not. Your father's plight is the same thing. His father was slain in the battle, so 'tis between him and us. Put on thy best clothes as fast as may be. Thou shalt have my wedding-veil and miniver mantle. Speed, I say. My lord has to hasten away to join the Earl on the way to London. He will see the knot tied beyond loosing at once."

To dress herself was all poor Grisell could do in her bewilderment. Remonstrance was vain. The actual marriage without choice was not so repugnant to all her feelings as to a modern maiden; it was the ordinary destiny of womanhood, and she had been used in her childhood to look on Leonard Copeland as her property; but to be forced on the poor youth instantly on his father's death, and as an alternative to execution, set all her maidenly feelings in revolt. Bernard was sitting up in bed, crying out that he could not lose his Grisly. Her mother was running backwards and forwards, bringing portions of her own bridal gear, and directing Thora, who was combing out her young lady's hair, which was long, of a beautiful brown, and was to be worn loose and flowing, in the bridal fashion. Grisell longed to kneel and pray, but her mother hurried her. "My lord must not be kept waiting, there would be time enough for prayer in the church." Then Bernard, clamouring loudly, threw his arms round the thick old heavy silken gown that had been put on her, and declared that he would not part with his Grisly, and his mother tore him away by force, declaring that he need not fear, Copeland would be in no hurry to take her away, and again when she bent to kiss him he clung tight round her neck almost strangling her, and rumpling her tresses.

Ridley had come up to say that my lord was calling for the young lady, and it was he who took the boy off and held him in his arms, as the mother, who seemed endued with new strength by the excitement, threw a large white muffling veil over Grisell's head and shoulders, and led or rather dragged her down to the hall.

The first sounds she there heard were, "Sir, I have given my faith to the Lady Eleanor of Audley, whom I love."

"What is that to me? 'Twas a precontract to my daughter."

"Not made by me nor her."

"By your parents, with myself. You went near to being her death outright, marred her face for life, so that none other will wed her. What say you? Not hurt by your own will? Who said it was? What matters that?"

"Sir," said Leonard, "it is true that by mishap, nay, if you will have it so, by a child's inadvertence, I caused this evil chance to befall your daughter, but I deny, and my father denies likewise, that there was any troth plight between the maid and me. She will own the same if you ask her. As I spake before, there was talk of the like kind between you, sir, and my father, and it was the desire of the good King that thus the families might be reconciled; but the contract went no farther, as the holy King himself owned when I gave my faith to the Lord Audley's daughter, and with it my heart."

"Aye, we know that the Frenchwoman can make the poor fool of a King believe and avouch anything she choose! This is not the point. No more words, young man. Here stands my daughter; there is the rope. Choose - wed or hang."

Leonard stood one moment with a look of agonised perplexity over his face. Then he said, "If I consent, am I at liberty, free at once to depart?"

"Aye," said Whitburn. "So you fulfil your contract, the rest is nought to me."

"I am then at liberty? Free to carry my sword to my

Queen and King?"

"Free."

"You swear it, on the holy cross?"

Lord Whitburn held up the cross hilt of his sword before him, and made oath on it that when once married to his daughter, Leonard Copeland was no longer his prisoner.

Grisell through her veil read on the youthful face a look of grief and renunciation; he was sacrificing his love to the needs of King and country, and his words chimed in with her conviction.

"Sir, I am ready. If it were myself alone, I would die rather than be false to my love, but my Queen needs good swords and faithful hearts, and I may not fail her. I am ready!"

"It is well!" said Lord Whitburn. "Ho, you there! Bring the horses to the door."

Grisell, in all the strange suspense of that decision, had been thinking of Sir Gawaine, whose lines rang in her head, but that look of grief roused other feelings. Sir Gawaine had no other love to sacrifice.

"Sir! sir!" she cried, as her father turned to bid her mount the pillion behind Ridley. "Can you not let him go free without? I always looked to a cloister."

"That is for you and he to settle, girl. Obey me now, or it will be the worse for him and you."

"One word I would say," added the mother. "How far hath this matter with the Audley maid gone? There is no troth plight, I trow?"

"No, by all that is holy, no. Would the lad not have pleaded it if there had been? No more dilly-dallying. Up on the horse, Grisly, and have done with it. We will show the young recreant how promises are kept in Durham County."

He dragged rather than led his daughter to the door, and lifted her passively to the pillion seat behind Cuthbert Ridley. A fine horse, Copeland's own, was waiting for him. He was allowed to ride freely, but old Whitburn kept close beside him, so that escape would have been impossible. He was in the armour in which he had fought, dimmed and dust-stained, but still glancing in the morning sun, which glittered on the sea, though a heavy western thunder-cloud, purple in the sun, was rising in front of this strange bridal cavalcade.

It was overhead by the time the church was reached, and the heavy rain that began to fall caused the priest to bid the whole party come within for the part of the ceremony usually performed outside the west door.

It was very dark within. The windows were small and old, and filled with dusky glass, and the arches were low browed. Grisell's mufflings were thrown aside, and she stood as became a maiden bride, with all her hair flowing over her shoulders and long tresses over her face, but even without this, her features would hardly have been visible, as the dense cloud rolled overhead; and indeed so tall and straight was her figure that no one would have supposed her other than a fair

Charlotte M. Yonge

young spouse. She trembled a good deal, but was too much terrified and, as it were, stunned for tears, and she durst not raise her drooping head even to look at her bridegroom, though such light as came in shone upon his fair hair and was reflected on his armour, and on one golden spur that still he wore, the other no doubt lost in the fight.

All was done regularly. The Lord of Whitburn was determined that no ceremony that could make the wedlock valid should be omitted. The priest, a kind old man, but of peasant birth, and entirely subservient to the Dacres, proceeded to ask each of the pair when they had been assoiled, namely, absolved. Grisell, as he well knew, had been shriven only last Friday; Leonard muttered, "Three days since, when I was dubbed knight, ere the battle."

"That suffices," put in the Baron impatiently. "On with you, Sir Lucas."

The thoroughly personal parts of the service were in English, and Grisell could not but look up anxiously when the solemn charge was given to mention whether there was any lawful "letting" to their marriage. Her heart bounded as it were to her throat when Leonard made no answer.

But then what lay before him if he pleaded his promise!

It went on - those betrothal vows, dictated while the two cold hands were linked, his with a kind of limp passiveness, hers, quaking, especially as, in the old use of York, he took her "for laither for fairer" - laith being equivalent to loathly - "till death us do part." And with failing heart, but still resolute heart, she faltered out her vow to cleave to him "for better for worse, for richer for poorer, in sickness or health, and to be bonner (debonair or cheerful) and boughsome (obedient) till that final parting."

The troth was plighted, and the silver mark - poor Leonard's sole available property at the moment - laid on the priest's book, as the words were said, "with worldly cathel I thee endow," and the ring, an old one of her mother's, was held on Grisell's finger. It was done, though, alas! the bridegroom could hardly say with truth, "with my body I thee worship."

Then followed the procession to the altar, the chilly hands barely touching one another, and the mass was celebrated, when Latin did not come home to the pair like English, though both fairly understood it. Grisell's feeling was by this time concentrated in the one hope that she should be dutiful to the poor, unwilling bridegroom, far more to be pitied than herself, and that she should be guarded by God whatever befell.

It was over. Signing of registers was not in those days, but there was some delay, for the darkness was more dense than ever, the rush of furious hail was heard without, a great blue flash of intense light filled every corner of the church, the thunder pealed so sharply and vehemently overhead that the small company looked at one another and at the church, to ascertain that no stroke had fallen. Then the Lord of Whitburn, first recovering himself, cried, "Come, sir knight, kiss your bride. Ha! where is he? Sir Leonard - here. Who hath seen him? Not vanished in yon flash! Eh?"

No, but the men without, cowering under the wall,

deposed that Sir Leonard Copeland had rushed out, shouted to them that he had fulfilled the conditions and was a free man, taken his horse, and galloped away through the storm.

CHAPTER XIV

THE LONELY BRIDE

Grace for the callant
If he marries our muckle-mouth Meg.

BROWNING.

"The recreant! Shall we follow him?" was the cry of Lord Whitburn's younger squire, Harry Featherstone, with his hand on his horse's neck, in spite of the torrents of rain and the fresh flash that set the horses quivering.

"No! no!" roared the Baron. "I tell you no! He has fulfilled his promise; I fulfil mine. He has his freedom. Let him go! For the rest, we will find the way to make him good husband to you, my wench," and as Harry murmured something, "There's work enow in hand without spending our horses' breath and our own in chasing after a runaway groom. A brief space we will wait till the storm be over."

Grisell shrank back to pray at a little side altar, telling her beads, and repeating the Latin formula, but in her heart all the time giving thanks that she was going back to Bernard and her mother, whose needs had been pressing strongly on her, yet that she might do right by

Charlotte M. Yonge

this newly-espoused husband, whose downcast, dejected look had filled her, not with indignation at the slight to her - she was far past that - but with yearning compassion for one thus severed from his true love.

When the storm had subsided enough for these hardy northlanders to ride home, and Grisell was again perched behind old Cuthbert Ridley, he asked, "Well, my Dame of Copeland, dost peak and pine for thy runaway bridegroom?"

"Nay, I had far rather be going home to my little Bernard than be away with yonder stranger I ken not whither."

"Thou art in the right, my wench. If the lad can break the marriage by pleading precontract, you may lay your reckoning on it that so he will."

When they came home to the attempt at a marriage-feast which Lady Whitburn had improvised, they found that this was much her opinion.

"He will get the knot untied," she said. "So thick as the King and his crew are with the Pope, it will cost him nothing, but we may, for very shame, force a dowry out of his young knighthood to get the wench into Whitby withal!"

"So he even proffered on his way," said the Baron. "He is a fair and knightly youth. 'Tis pity of him that he holds with the Frenchwoman. Ha, Bernard, 'tis for thy good."

For the boy was clinging tight to his sister, and declaring that his Grisly should never leave him again, not for twenty vile runaway husbands.

Grisell returned to all her old habits, and there was no difference in her position, excepting that she was scrupulously called Dame Grisell Copeland. Her father was soon called away by the summons to Parliament, sent forth in the name of King Henry, who was then in the hands of the Earl of Warwick in London. The Sheriff's messenger who brought him the summons plainly said that all the friends of York, Salisbury, and Warwick were needed for a great change that would dash the hopes of the Frenchwoman and her son.

He went with all his train, leaving the defence of the castle to Ridley and the ladies, and assuring Grisell that she need not be downhearted. He would yet bring her fine husband, Sir Leonard, to his marrow bones before her.

Grisell had not much time to think of Sir Leonard, for as the summer waned, both her mother and Bernard sickened with low fever. In the lady's case it was intermittent, and she spent only the third day in her bed, the others in crouching over the fire or hanging over the child's bed, where he lay constantly tossing and fevered all night, sometimes craving to be on his sister's lap, but too restless long to lie there. Both manifestly became weaker, in spite of all Grisell's simple treatment, and at last she wrung from the lady permission to send Ridley to Wearmouth to try if it was possible to bring out Master Lambert Groot to give his advice, or if not, to obtain medicaments and counsel from him.

The good little man actually came, riding a mule. "Ay, ay," quoth Ridley, "I brought him, though he vowed at first it might never be, but when he heard it concerned you, mistress - I mean Dame Grisell - he was ready to come to your aid."

Good little man, standing trim and neat in his burgher's dress and little frill-like ruff, he looked quite out of place in the dark old hall.

Lady Whitburn seemed to think him a sort of magician, though inferior enough to be under her orders. "Ha! Is that your Poticary?" she demanded, when Grisell brought him up to the solar. "Look at my bairn, Master Dutchman; see to healing him," she continued imperiously.

Lambert was too well used to incivility from nobles to heed her manner, though in point of fact a Flemish noble was far more civilised than this North Country dame. He looked anxiously at Bernard, who moaned a little and turned his head away. "Nay, now, Bernard," entreated his sister; "look up at the good man, he that sent you the sugar-balls. He is come to try to make you well."

Bernard let her coax him to give his poor little wasted hand to the leech, and looked with wonder in his heavy eyes at the stranger, who felt his pulse, and asked to have him lifted up for better examination. There was at first a dismal little whine at being touched and moved, but when a pleasantly acid drop was put into his little parched mouth, he smiled with brief content. His mother evidently expected that both he and she herself would be relieved on the spot, but the Apothecary durst not be hopeful, though he gave the child a draught which he called a febrifuge, and which put him to sleep, and bade the lady take another of the like if she wished for a good night's rest.

He added, however, that the best remedy would be a pilgrimage to Lindisfarne, which, be it observed, really meant absence from the foul, close, feverish air of the castle, and all the evil odours of the court. To the lady he thought it would really be healing, but he doubted whether the poor little boy was not too far gone for such revival; indeed, he made no secret that he believed the child was stricken for death.

"Then what boots all your vaunted chirurgery!" cried the mother passionately. "You outlandish cheat! you! What did you come here for? You have not even let him blood!"

"Let him blood! good madame," exclaimed Master Lambert. "In his state, to take away his blood would be to kill him outright!"

"False fool and pretender," cried Lady Whitburn; "as if all did not ken that the first duty of a leech is to take away the infected humours of the blood! Demented as I was to send for you. Had you been worth but a pinch of salt, you would have shown me how to lay hands on Nan the witch-wife, the cause of all the scathe to my poor bairn."

Master Lambert could only protest that he laid no claim to the skill of a witch-finder, whereupon the lady stormed at him as having come on false pretences, and at her daughter for having brought him, and finally fell into a paroxysm of violent weeping, during which Grisell was thankful to convey her guest out of the chamber, and place him under the care of Ridley, who would take care he had food and rest, and safe convoy

Charlotte M. Yonge

back to Wearmouth when his mule had been rested and baited.

"Oh, Master Lambert," she said, "it grieves me that you should have been thus treated."

"Heed not that, sweet lady. It oft falls to our share to brook the like, and I fear me that yours is a weary lot."

"But my brother! my little brother!" she asked. "It is all out of my mother's love for him."

"Alack, lady, what can I say? The child is sickly, and little enough is there of peace or joy in this world for such, be he high or low born. Were it not better that the Saints should take him to their keeping, while yet a sackless babe?"

Grisell wrung her hands together. "Ah! he hath been all my joy or bliss through these years; but I will strive to say it is well, and yield my will."

The crying of the poor little sufferer for his Grisly called her back before she could say or hear more. Her mother lay still utterly exhausted on her bed, and hardly noticed her; but all that evening, and all the ensuing night, Grisell held the boy, sometimes on her lap, sometimes on the bed, while all the time his moans grew more and more feeble, his words more indistinct. By and by, as she sat on the bed, holding him on her breast, he dropped asleep, and perhaps, outwearied as she was, she slept too. At any rate all was still, till she was roused by a cry from Thora, "Holy St. Hilda! the bairn has passed!"

And indeed when Grisell started, the little head and

hand that had been clasped to her fell utterly prone, and there was a strange cold at her breast.

Her mother woke with a loud wail. "My bairn! My bairn!" snatching him to her arms. "This is none other than your Dutchman's doings, girl. Have him to the dungeon! Where are the stocks? Oh, my pretty boy! He breathed, he is living. Give me the wine!" Then as there was no opening of the pale lips, she fell into another tempest of tears, during which Grisell rushed to the stair, where on the lowest step she met Lambert and Ridley.

"Have him away! Have him away, Cuthbert," she cried. "Out of the castle instantly. My mother is distraught with grief; I know not what she may do to him. O go! Not a word!"

They could but obey, riding away in the early morning, and leaving the castle to its sorrow.

So, tenderly and sadly was little Bernard carried to the vault in the church, while Grisell knelt as his chief mourner, for her mother, after her burst of passion subsided, lay still and listless, hardly noticing anything, as if there had fallen on her some stroke that affected her brain. Tidings of the Baron were slow to come, and though Grisell sent a letter by a wandering friar to York, with information of the child's death and the mother's illness, it was very doubtful when or whether they would ever reach him.

CHAPTER XV

WAKEFIELD BRIDGE

I come to tell you things since then befallen.
After the bloody fray at Wakefield fought,
Where your brave father breathed his latest gasp.

SHAKESPEARE, King Henry VI., Part III.

Christmas went by sadly in Whitburn Tower, but the succeeding weeks were to be sadder still. It was on a long dark evening that a commotion was heard at the gate, and Lady Whitburn, who had been sitting by the smouldering fire in her chamber, seemed suddenly startled into life.

"Tidings," she cried. "News of my lord and son. Bring them, Grisell, bring them up."

Grisell obeyed, and hurried down to the hall. All the household, men and maids, were gathered round some one freshly come in, and the first sound she heard was, "Alack! Alack, my lady!"

"How - what - how -" she asked breathlessly, just recognising Harry Featherstone, pale, dusty, blood-stained.

"It is evil news, dear lady," said old Ridley, turning towards her with outstretched hands, and tears flowing down his cheeks. "My knight. Oh! my knight! And I was not by!"

"Slain?" almost under her breath, asked Grisell.

"Even so! At Wakefield Bridge," began Featherstone, but at that instant, walking stiff, upright, and rigid, like a figure moved by mechanism, Lady Whitburn was among them.

"My lord," she said, still as if her voice belonged to some one else. "Slain? And thou, recreant, here to tell the tale!"

"Madam, he fell before I had time to strike." She seemed to hear no word, but again demanded, "My son."

He hesitated a moment, but she fiercely reiterated.

"My son! Speak out, thou coward loon."

"Madam, Robert was cut down by the Lord Clifford beside the Earl of Rutland. 'Tis a lost field! I barely 'scaped with a dozen men. I came but to bear the tidings, and see whether you needed an arm to hold out the castle for young Bernard. Or I would be on my way to my own folk on the Border, for the Queen's men will anon be everywhere, since the Duke is slain!"

"The Duke! The Duke of York!" was the cry, as if a tower were down.

" What would you. We were caught by Somerset like

deer in a buck-stall. Here! Give me a cup of ale, I can scarce speak for chill."

He sank upon the settle as one quite worn out. The ale was brought by some one, and he drank a long draught, while, at a sign from Ridley, one of the serving-men began to draw off his heavy boots and greaves, covered with frosted mud, snow, and blood, all melting together, but all the time he talked, and the hearers remained stunned and listening to what had hardly yet penetrated their understanding. Lady Whitburn had collapsed into her own chair, and was as still as the rest.

He spoke incoherently, and Ridley now and then asked a question, but his fragmentary narrative may be thus expanded.

All had, in Yorkist opinion, gone well in London. Henry was in the power of the White Rose, and had actually consented that Richard of York should be his next heir, but in the meantime Queen Margaret had been striving her utmost to raise the Welsh and the Border lords on behalf of her son. She had obtained aid from Scotland, and the Percies, the Dacres of Gilsland, and many more, had followed her standard. The Duke of York and Earl of Salisbury set forth to repress what they called a riot, probably unaware of the numbers who were daily joining the Queen. With them went Lord Whitburn, hoping thence to return home, and his son Robert, still a squire of the Duke's household.

They reached York's castle of Sendal, and there merrily kept Christmas, but on St. Thomas of Canterbury's Day they heard that the foe were close at hand, many thousands strong, and on the morrow

Queen Margaret, with her boy beside her, and the Duke of Somerset, came before the gate and called on the Duke to surrender the castle, and his own vaunting claims with it, or else come out and fight.

Sir Davy Hall entreated the Duke to remain in the castle till his son Edward, Earl of March, could bring reinforcements up from Wales, but York held it to be dishonourable to shut himself up on account of a scolding woman, and the prudence of the Earl of Salisbury was at fault, since both presumed on the easy victories they had hitherto gained. Therefore they sallied out towards Wakefield Bridge, to confront the main body of Margaret's army, ignorant or careless that she had two wings in reserve. These closed in on them, and their fate was certain.

"My lord fell in the melee among the first," said Featherstone. "I was down beside him, trying to lift him up, when a big Scot came with his bill and struck at my head, and I knew no more till I found my master lying stark dead and stripped of all his armour. My sword was gone, but I got off save for this cut" (and he pushed back his hair) "and a horse's kick or two, for the whole battle had gone over me, and I heard the shouting far away. As my lord lay past help, methought I had best shift myself ere more rascaille came to strip the slain. And as luck or my good Saint would have it, as I stumbled among the corpses I heard a whinnying, and saw mine own horse, Brown Weardale, running masterless. Glad enough was he, poor brute, to have my hand on his rein.

"The bridge was choked with fighting men, so I was about to put him to the river, when whom should I see on the bridge but young Master Robin, and with him young Lord Edmund of Rutland. There, on the other side, holding parley with them, was the knight Mistress Grisell wedded, and though he wore the White Rose, he gave his hand to them, and was letting them go by in safety. I was calling to Master Rob to let me pass as one of his own, when thundering on came the grim Lord Clifford, roaring like the wind in Roker caves. I heard him howl at young Copeland for a traitor, letting go the accursed spoilers of York. Copeland tried to speak, but Clifford dashed him aside against the wall, and, ah! woe's me, lady, when Master Robin threw himself between, the fellow - a murrain on his name - ran the fair youth through the neck with his sword, and swept him off into the river. Then he caught hold of Lord Edmund, crying out, "Thy father slew mine, and so do I thee," and dashed out his brains with his mace. For me, I rode along farther, swam my horse over the river in the twilight, with much ado to keep clear of the dead horses and poor slaughtered comrades that cumbered the stream, and what was even worse, some not yet dead, borne along and crying out. A woful day it was to all who loved the kindly Duke of York, or this same poor house! As luck would have it, I fell in with Jock of Redesdale and a few more honest fellows, who had 'scaped. We found none but friends when we were well past the river. They succoured us at the first abbey we came to. The rest have sped to their homes, and here am I."

Such was the tenor of Featherstone's doleful history of that blood-thirsty Lancastrian victory. All had hung in dire suspense on his words, and not till they were ended did Grisell become conscious that her mother was sitting like a stone, with fixed, glassy eyes and dropped lip, in the high-backed chair, quite senseless, and breathing strangely.

They took her up and carried her upstairs, as one who had received her death stroke as surely as had her husband and son on the slopes between Sendal and Wakefield.

Grisell and Thora did their utmost, but without reviving her, and they watched by her, hardly conscious of anything else, as they tried their simple, ineffective remedies one after another, with no thought or possibility of sending for further help, since the roads would be impassable in the long January night, and besides, the Lancastrians might make them doubly perilous. Moreover, this dumb paralysis was accepted as past cure, and needing not the doctor but the priest. Before the first streak of dawn on that tardy, northern morning, Ridley's ponderous step came up the stair, into the feeble light of the rush candle which the watchers tried to shelter from the draughts.

The sad question and answer of "No change" passed, and then Ridley, his gruff voice unnecessarily hushed, said, "Featherstone would speak with you, lady. He would know whether it be your pleasure to keep him in your service to hold out the Tower, or whether he is free to depart."

"Mine!" said Grisell bewildered.

"Yea!" exclaimed Ridley. "You are Lady of Whitburn!"

"Ah! It is true," exclaimed Grisell, clasping her hands. "Woe is me that it should be so! And oh! Cuthbert! my husband, if he lives, is a Queen's man! What can I do?"

"If it were of any boot I would say hold out the Tower.

Charlotte M. Yonge

He deserves no better after the scurvy way he treated you," said Cuthbert grimly. "He may be dead, too, though Harry fears he was but stunned."

"But oh!" cried Grisell, as if she saw one gleam of light, "did not I hear something of his trying to save my brother and Lord Edmund?"

"You had best come down and hear," said Ridley. "Featherstone cannot go till he has spoken with you, and he ought to depart betimes, lest the Gilsland folk and all the rest of them be ravening on their way back."

Grisell looked at her mother, who lay in the same state, entirely past her reach. The hard, stern woman, who had seemed to have no affection to bestow on her daughter, had been entirely broken down and crushed by the loss of her sons and husband.

Probably neither had realised that by forcing Grisell on young Copeland they might be giving their Tower to their enemy.

She went down to the hall, where Harry Featherstone, whose night had done him more good than hers had, came to meet her, looking much freshened, and with a bandage over his forehead. He bent low before her, and offered her his services, but, as he told her, he and Ridley had been talking it over, and they thought it vain to try to hold out the Tower, even if any stout men did straggle back from the battle, for the country round was chiefly Lancastrian, and it would be scarcely possible to get provisions, or to be relieved. Moreover, the Gilsland branch of the family, who would be the male heirs, were on the side of the King and Queen, and might drive her out if she resisted. Thus there seemed no occasion for the squire to remain, and he hoped to reach his own family, and save himself from the risk of being captured.

"No, sir, we do not need you," said Grisell. "If Sir Leonard Copeland lives and claims this Tower, there is no choice save to yield it to him. I would not delay you in seeking your own safety, but only thank you for your true service to my lord and father."

She held out her hand, which Featherstone kissed on his knee.

His horse was terribly jaded, and he thought he could make his way more safely on foot than in the panoply of an esquire, for in this war, the poorer sort were hardly touched; the attacks were chiefly made on nobles and gentlemen. So he prepared to set forth, but Grisell obtained from him what she had scarcely understood the night before, the entire history of the fall of her father and brother, and how gallantly Leonard Copeland had tried to withstand Clifford's rage.

"He did his best for them," she said, as if it were her one drop of hope and comfort.

Ridley very decidedly hoped that Clifford's blow had freed her from her reluctant husband; and mayhap the marriage would give her claims on the Copeland property. But Grisell somehow could not join in the wish. She could only remember the merry boy at Amesbury and the fair face she had seen sleeping in the hall, and she dwelt on Featherstone's assurance that no wound had pierced the knight, and that he would probably be little the worse for his fall against the parapet of the bridge. Use her as he might, she could not wish him dead, though it was a worthy death in defence of his old playfellow and of her own brother.

CHAPTER XVI

A NEW MASTER

In the dark chambere, if the bride was fair,
Ye wis, I could not see.
. . . .
And the bride rose from her knee
And kissed the smile of her mother dead.

E. B. BROWNING, The Romaunt of the Page.

The Lady of Whitburn lingered from day to day, sometimes showing signs of consciousness, and of knowing her daughter, but never really reviving. At the end of a fortnight she seemed for one day somewhat better, but that night she had a fresh attack, and was so evidently dying that the priest, Sir Lucas, was sent for to bring her the last Sacrament. The passing bell rang out from the church, and the old man, with his little server before him, came up the stair, and was received by Grisell, Thora, and one or two other servants on their knees.

Ridley was not there. For even then, while the priest was crossing the hall, a party of spearmen, with a young knight at their head, rode to the gate and demanded entrance.

Charlotte M. Yonge

The frightened porter hurried to call Master Ridley, who, instead of escorting the priest with the Host to his dying lady, had to go to the gate, where he recognised Sir Leonard Copeland, far from dead, in very different guise from that in which he had been brought to the castle before. He looked, however, awed, as he said, bending his head -

"Is it sooth, Master Ridley? Is death beforehand with me?"

"My old lady is in extremis, sir," replied Ridley. "Poor soul, she hath never spoken since she heard of my lord's death and his son's."

"The younger lad? Lives here?" demanded Copeland. "Is it as I have heard?"

"Aye, sir. The child passed away on the Eve of St. Luke. I have my lady's orders," he added reluctantly, "to open the castle to you, as of right."

"It is well," returned Sir Leonard. Then, turning round to the twenty men who followed him, he said, "Men-at-arms, as you saw and heard, there is death here. Draw up here in silence. This good esquire will see that you have food and fodder for the horses. Kemp, Hardcastle," to his squires, "see that all is done with honour and respect as to the lady of the castle and mine. Aught unseemly shall be punished."

Wherewith he dismounted, and entered the narrow little court, looking about him with a keen, critical, soldierly eye, but speaking with low, grave tones.

"I may not tarry," he said to Ridley, "but this place,

since it falls to me and mine, must be held for the King and Queen."

"My lady bows to your will, sir," returned Ridley.

Copeland continued to survey the walls and very antiquated defences, observing that there could have been few alarms there. This lasted till the rites in the sick-room were ended, and the priest came forth.

"Sir," he said to Copeland, "you will pardon the young lady. Her mother is in articulo mortis, and she cannot leave her."

"I would not disturb her," said Leonard. "The Saints forbid that I should vex her. I come but as in duty bound to damn this Tower on behalf of King Harry, Queen Margaret, and the Prince of Wales against all traitors. I will not tarry here longer than to put it into hands who will hold it for them and for me. How say you, Sir Squire?" he added, turning to Ridley, not discourteously.

"We ever did hold for King Harry, sir," returned the old esquire.

"Yea, but against his true friends, York and Warwick. One is cut off, ay, and his aider and defender, Salisbury, who should rather have stood by his King, has suffered a traitor's end at Pomfret."

"My Lord of Salisbury! Ah! that will grieve my poor young lady," sighed Ridley.

"He was a kind lord, save for his treason to the King," said Leonard. "We of his household long ago were happy enough, though strangely divided now. For the rest, till that young wolf cub, Edward of March, and his mischief-stirring cousin of Warwick be put down, this place must be held against them and theirs - whosoever bears the White Rose. Wilt do so, Master Seneschal?"

"I hold for my lady. That is all I know," said Ridley, "and she holds herself bound to you, sir."

"Faithful. Ay? You will be her guardian, I see; but I must leave half a score of fellows for the defence, and will charge them that they show all respect and honour to the lady, and leave to you, as seneschal, all the household, and of all save the wardship of the Tower, calling on you first to make oath of faith to me, and to do nought to the prejudice of King Henry, the Queen, or Prince, nor to favour the friends of York or Warwick."

"I am willing, sir," returned Ridley, who cared a great deal more for the house of Whitburn than for either party, whose cause he by no means understood, perhaps no more than they had hitherto done themselves. As long as he was left to protect his lady it was all he asked, and more than he expected, and the courtesy, not to say delicacy, of the young knight greatly impressed both him and the priest, though he suspected that it was a relief to Sir Leonard not to be obliged to see his bride of a few months.

The selected garrison were called in. Ridley would rather have seen them more of the North Country yeoman type than of the regular weather-beaten men-at-arms whom wars always bred up; but their officer was a slender, dainty-looking, pale young squire, with his arm in a sling, named Pierce Hardcastle, selected apparently because his wound rendered rest desirable. Sir Leonard reiterated his charge that all honour and respect was to be paid to the Lady of Whitburn, and that she was free to come and go as she chose, and to be obeyed in every respect, save in what regarded the defence of the Tower. He himself was going on to Monks Wearmouth, where he had a kinsman among the monks.

With an effort, just as he remounted his horse, he said to Ridley, "Commend me to the lady. Tell her that I am grieved for her sorrow and to be compelled to trouble her at such a time; but 'tis for my Queen's service, and when this troublous times be ended, she shall hear more from me." Turning to the priest he added, "I have no coin to spare, but let all be done that is needed for the souls of the departed lord and lady, and I will be answerable."

Nothing could be more courteous, but as he rode off priest and squire looked at one another, and Ridley said, "He will untie your knot, Sir Lucas."

"He takes kindly to castle and lands," was the answer, with a smile; "they may make the lady to be swallowed."

"I trow 'tis for his cause's sake," replied Ridley. "Mark you, he never once said 'My lady,' nor 'My wife.'"

"May the sweet lady come safely out of it any way," sighed the priest. "She would fain give herself and her lands to the Church."

"May be 'tis the best that is like to befall her," said Ridley; "but if that young featherpate only had the wit to guess it, he would find that he might seek Christendom over for a better wife."

They were interrupted by a servant, who came hurrying down to say that my lady was even now departing, and to call Sir Lucas to the bedside.

All was over a few moments after he reached the apartment, and Grisell was left alone in her desolation. The only real, deep, mutual love had been between her and poor little Bernard; her elder brother she had barely seen; her father had been indifferent, chiefly regarding her as a damaged piece of property, a burthen to the estate; her mother had been a hard, masculine, untender woman, only softened in her latter days by the dependence of ill health and her passion for her sickly youngest; but on her Grisell had experienced Sister Avice's lesson that ministry to others begets and fosters love.

And now she was alone in her house, last of her household, her work for her mother over, a wife, but loathed and deserted except so far as that the tie had sanctioned the occupation of her home by a hostile garrison. Her spirit sank within her, and she bitterly felt the impoverishment of the always scanty means, which deprived her of the power of laying out sums of money on those rites which were universally deemed needful for the repose of souls snatched away in battle. It was a mercenary age among the clergy, and besides, it was the depth of a northern winter, and the funeral rites of the Lady of Whitburn would have been poor and maimed indeed if a whole band of black Benedictine monks had not arrived from Wearmouth, saying they had been despatched at special request and charge of Sir Leonard Copeland.

CHAPTER XVII

STRANGE GUESTS

The needle, having nought to do,
Was pleased to let the magnet wheedle,
Till closer still the tempter drew,
And off at length eloped the needle.

T. MOORE.

The nine days of mourning were spent in entire seclusion by Grisell, who went through every round of devotions prescribed or recommended by the Church, and felt relief and rest in them. She shrank when Ridley on the tenth day begged her no longer to seclude herself in the solar, but to come down to the hall and take her place as Lady of the Castle, otherwise he said he could not answer for the conduct of Copeland's men.

"Master Hardcastle desires it too," he said. "He is a good lad enough, but I doubt me whether his hand is strong enough over those fellows! You need not look for aught save courtesy from him! Come down, lady, or you will never have your rights."

"Ah, Cuthbert, what are my rights?"

"To be mistress of your own castle," returned Ridley, "and that you will never be unless you take the upper hand. Here are all our household eating with these rogues of Copeland's, and who is to keep rule if the lady comes not?"

"Alack, and how am I to do so?"

However, the consideration brought her to appear at the very early dinner, the first meal of the day, which followed on the return from mass. Pierce Hardcastle met her shyly. He was a tall slender stripling, looking weak and ill, and he bowed very low as he said, "Greet you well, lady," and looked up for a moment as if in fear of what he might encounter. Grisell indeed was worn down with long watching and grief, and looked haggard and drawn so as to enhance all her scars and distortion of feature into more uncomeliness than her wont. She saw him shudder a little, but his lame arm and wan looks interested her kind heart. "I fear me you are still feeling your wound, sir," she said, in the sweet voice which was evidently a surprise to him.

"It is my plea for having been a slug-a-bed this morning," he answered.

They sat down at the table. Grisell between Ridley and Hardcastle, the servants and men-at-arms beyond. Porridge and broth and very small ale were the fare, and salted meat would be for supper, and as Grisell knew but too well already, her own retainers were grumbling at the voracious appetites of the men-at-arms as much as did their unwilling guests at the plainness and niggardliness of the supply.

Thora had begged for a further allowance of beer for

them, or even to broach a cask of wine. "For," said she, "they are none such fiends as we thought, if one knows how to take them courteously."

"There is no need that you should have any dealings with them, Thora," said her lady, with some displeasure; "Master Ridley sees to their provision."

Thora tossed up her head a little and muttered something about not being mewed out of sight and speech of all men. And when she attended her lady to the hall there certainly were glances between her and a slim young archer.

The lady's presence was certainly a restraint on the rude men-at-arms, though two or three of them seemed to her rough, reckless-looking men. After the meal all her kindly instincts were aroused to ask what she could do for the young squire, and he willingly put himself into her hands, for his hurt had become much more painful within the last day or two, as indeed it proved to be festering, and in great need of treatment.

Before the day was over the two had made friends, and Grisell had found him to be a gentle, scholarly youth, whom the defence of the Queen had snatched from his studies into the battlefield. He told her a great deal about the good King, and his encouragement of his beloved scholars at Eton, and he spoke of Queen Margaret with an enthusiasm new to Grisell, who had only heard her reviled as the Frenchwoman. Pierce could speak with the greatest admiration, too, of his own knight, Sir Leonard, whom he viewed as the pink of chivalry, assuring Lady Copeland, as he called her, that she need never doubt for a moment of his true honour and courtesy. Grisell longed to know, but modest pride forbade her to ask, whether he knew how matters stood with her rival, Lady Eleanor Audley. Ridley, however, had no such feeling, and he reported to Grisell what he had discovered.

Young Hardcastle had only once seen the lady, and had thought her very beautiful, as she looked from a balcony when King Henry was riding to his Parliament. Leonard Copeland, then a squire, was standing beside her, and it had been currently reported that he was to be her bridegroom.

He had returned from his captivity after the battle of Northampton exceedingly downcast, but striving vehemently in the cause of Lancaster, and Hardcastle had heard that the question had been discussed whether the forced marriage had been valid, or could be dissolved; but since the bodies of Lord Whitburn and his son had been found on the ground at Wakefield, this had ceased, and it was believed that Queen Margaret had commanded Sir Leonard, on his allegiance, to go and take possession of Whitburn and its vassals in her cause.

But Pierce Hardcastle had come to Ridley's opinion, that did his knight but shut his eyes, the Lady Grisell was as good a mate as man could wish both in word and deed.

"I would fain," said he, "have the Lady Eleanor to look at, but this lady to dress my hurts, ay, and talk with me. Never met I woman who was so good company! She might almost be a scholar at Oxford for her wit."

However much solace the lady might find in the courtesy of Master Hardcastle, she was not pleased to find that her hand-maiden Thora exchanged glances with the young men-at-arms; and in a few days Ridley spoke to Grisell, and assured her that mischief would ensue if the silly wench were not checked in her habit of loitering and chattering whenever she could escape from her lady's presence in the solar, which Grisell used as her bower, only descending to the hall at meal-times.

Grisell accordingly rebuked her the next time she delayed unreasonably over a message, but the girl pouted and muttered something about young Ralph Hart helping her with the heavy pitcher up the stair.

"It is unseemly for a maiden to linger and get help from strange soldiers," said Grisell.

"No more unseemly than for the dame to be ever holding converse with their captain," retorted the North Country hand-maiden, free of speech and with a toss of the head.

"Whist, Thora! or you must take a buffet," said Grisell, clenching a fist unused to striking, and trying to regard chastisement as a duty. "You know full well that my only speech with Master Hardcastle is as his hostess."

Thora laughed. "Ay, lady; I ken well what the men say. How that poor youth is spell-bound, and that you are casting your glamour over him as of old over my poor old lady and little Master Bernard."

"For shame, Thora, to bring me such tales!" and Grisell's hand actually descended on her maiden's face, but so slight was the force that it only caused a contemptuous laugh, which so angered the young mistress as to give her energy to strike again with all her might.

"And you'd beat me," observed her victim, roused to anger. "You are so ill favoured yourself that you cannot bear a man to look on a fair maid!"

"What insolence is this?" cried Grisell, utterly amazed. "Go into the turret room, spin out this hank, and stay there till I call you to supper. Say your Ave, and recollect what beseems a modest maiden."

She spoke with authority, which Thora durst not resist, and withdrew still pouting and grumbling.

Grisell was indeed young herself and inexperienced, and knew not that her wrath with the girl might be perilous to herself, while sympathy might have evoked wholesome confidence.

For the maiden, just developing into northern comeliness, was attractive enough to win the admiration of soldiers in garrison with nothing to do, and on her side their notice, their rough compliments, and even their jests, were delightful compared with the dulness of her mistress's mourning chamber, and court enough was paid to her completely to turn her head. If there were love and gratitude lurking in the bottom of her heart towards the lady who had made a fair and skilful maiden out of the wild fisher girl, all was smothered in the first strong impulse of love for this young Ralph Hart, the first to awaken the woman out of the child.

The obstacles which Grisell, like other prudent mistresses in all times, placed in the course of this true love, did but serve to alienate the girl and place her in opposition. The creature had grown up as wild and untamed as one of the seals on the shore, and though she had had a little training and teaching of late years, it was entirely powerless when once the passion was evoked in her by the new intercourse and rough compliments of the young archer, and she was for the time at his beck and call, regarding her lady as her tyrant and enemy. It was the old story of many a household.

CHAPTER XVIII

WITCHERY

The lady has gone to her secret bower,
The bower that was guarded by word and by spell.

SCOTT, The Lay of the Last Minstrel.

"Master Squire," said the principal man-at-arms of the garrison to Pierce Hardcastle, "is it known to you what this laidly dame's practices be?"

"I know her for a dame worthy of all honour and esteem," returned the esquire, turning hastily round in wrath. He much disliked this man, a regular mercenary of the free lance description, a fellow of French or Alsatian birth, of middle age, much strength, and on account of a great gash and sideways twist of his snub nose always known as Tordu, and strongly suspected that he had been sent as a sort of spy or check on Sir Leonard Copeland and on himself. The man replied with a growl:

"Ah ha! Sans doubt she makes her niggard fare seem dainty cakes to those under her art."

In fact the evident pleasure young Hardcastle took in the Lady Castellane's society, the great improvement in

Charlotte M. Yonge

his wound under her treatment, and the manner in which the serfs around came to ask her aid in their maladies, had excited the suspicion of the men-at-arms. They were older men, hardened and roughened, inclined to despise his youth, and to resent the orderly discipline of the household, which under Ridley went on as before, and the murmurs of Thora led to inquiries, answered after the exaggerated fashion of gossip.

There were outcries about provisions and wine or ale, and shouts demanding more, and when Pierce declared that he would not have the lady insulted, there was a hoarse loud laugh. He was about to order Tordu as ringleader into custody, but Ridley said to him aside, "Best not, sir; his fellows will not lay a finger on him, and if we did so, there would be a brawl, and we might come by the worst."

So Pierce could only say, with all the force he could, "Bear in mind that Sir Leonard Copeland is lord here, and all miscourtesy to his lady is an offence to himself, which will be visited with his wrath."

The sneering laugh came again, and Tordu made answer, "Ay, ay, sir; she has bewitched you, and we'll soon have him and you free."

Pierce was angered into flying at the man with his sword, but the other men came between, and Ridley held him back.

"You are still a maimed man, sir. To be foiled would be worse than to let it pass."

"There, fellow, I'll spare you, so you ask pardon of me

and the lady."

Perhaps they thought they had gone too far, for there was a sulky growl that might pass for an apology, and Ridley's counsel was decided that Pierce had better not pursue the matter.

What had been said, however, alarmed him, and set him on the watch, and the next evening, when Hardcastle was walking along the cliffs beyond the castle, the lad who acted as his page came to him, with round, wondering eyes, "Sir," said he, after a little hesitation, "is it sooth that the lady spake a spell over your arm?"

"Not to my knowledge," said Pierce smiling.

"It might be without your knowledge," said the boy. "They say it healed as no chirurgeon could have healed it, and by magic arts."

"Ha! the lubbard oafs. You know better than to believe them, Dick."

"Nay, sir, but 'tis her bower-woman and Madge, the cook's wife. Both aver that the lady hath bewitched whoever comes in her way ever since she crossed the door. She hath wrought strange things with her father, mother, and brothers. They say she bound them to her; that the little one could not brook to have her out of sight; yet she worked on him so that he was crooked and shrivelled. Yet he wept and cried to have her ever with him, while he peaked and pined and dwindled away. And her mother, who was once a fine, stately, masterful dame, pined to mere skin and bone, and lay in lethargy; and now she is winding her charms on you, sir!"

Pierce made an exclamation of loathing and contempt. Dick lowered his voice to a whisper of awe.

"Nay, sir, but Le Tordu and Ned of the Bludgeon purpose to ride over to Shields to the wise, and they will deal with her when he has found the witch's mark."

"The lady!" cried Hardcastle in horror. "You see her what she is! A holy woman if ever there was one! At mass each morning."

"Ay, but the wench Thora told Ralph that 'tis prayers backward she says there. Thora has oft heard her at night, and 'twas no Ave nor Credo as they say them here."

Pierce burst out laughing. "I should think not. They speak gibberish, and she, for I have heard her in Church, speaks words with a meaning, as her priest and nuns taught her."

"But her face, sir. There's the Evil One's mark. One side says nay to the other."

"The Evil One! Nay, Dick, he is none other than Sir Leonard himself. 'Twas he that all unwittingly, when a boy, fired a barrel of powder close to her and marred her countenance. You are not fool and ass enough to give credence to these tales."

"I said not that I did, sir," replied the page; "but it is what the men-at-arms swear to, having drawn it from the serving-maid."

"The adder," muttered Pierce.

"Moreover," continued the boy, "they have found out that there is a wise man witch-finder at Shields. They mean to be revenged for the scanty fare and mean providings; and they deem it will be a merry jest in this weary hold, and that Sir Leonard will be too glad to be quit of his gruesome dame to call them to account."

It was fearful news, for Pierce well knew his own incompetence to restrain these strong and violent men. He did not know where his knight was to be found, and, if he had known, it was only too likely that these terrible intentions might be carried out before any messenger could reach him. Indeed, the belief in sorcery was universal, and no rank was exempt from the danger of the accusation. Thora's treachery was specially perilous. All that the young man could do was to seek counsel with Cuthbert Ridley, and even this he was obliged to do in the stable, bidding Dick keep watch outside. Ridley too had heard a spiteful whisper or two, but it had seemed too preposterous for him to attend to it. "You are young, Hardcastle," he said, with a smile, "or you would know that there is nothing a grumbler will not say, nor how far men's tongues lie from their hands."

"Nay, but if their hands DID begin to act, how should we save the lady? There's nothing Tordu would not do. Could we get her away to some nunnery?"

"There is no nunnery nearer at hand than Gateshead, and there the Prioress is a Musgrove, no friend to my lord. She might give her up, on such a charge, for holy Church is no guardian in them. My poor bairn! That ingrate Thora too! I would fain wring her neck! Yet here are our fisher folk, who love her for her bounty."

"Would they hide her?" asked Pierce.

"That serving-wench - would I had drowned her ere bringing her here - might turn them, and, were she tracked, I ken not who might not be scared or tortured into giving her up!"

Here Dick looked in. "Tordu is crossing the yard," he said.

They both became immediately absorbed in studying the condition of Featherstone's horse, which had never wholly recovered the flight from Wakefield.

After a time Ridley was able to steal away, and visit Grisell in her apartment. She came to meet him, and he read alarm, incredulous alarm, in her face. She put her hands in his. "Is it sooth?" she said, in a strange, awe-stricken voice.

"You have heard, then, my wench?"

"Thora speaks in a strange tone, as though evil were brewing against me. But you, and Master Hardcastle, and Sir Lucas, and the rest would never let them touch me?"

"They should only do so through my heart's blood, dear child; but mine would be soon shed, and Hardcastle is a weakly lad, whom those fellows believe to be bewitched. We must find some other way!"

"Sir Leonard would save me if he knew. Alas! the good Earl of Salisbury is dead."

"'Tis true. If we could hide you till we be rid of these men. But where?" and he made a despairing gesture.

Grisell stood stunned and dazed as the horrible prospect rose before her of being seized by these lawless men, tortured by the savage hands of the witch-finder, subjected to a cruel death, by fire, or at best by water. She pressed her hands together, feeling utterly desolate, and prayed her prayer to the God of the fatherless to save her or brace her to endure.

Presently Cuthbert exclaimed, "Would Master Groats, the Poticary, shelter you till this is over-past? His wife is deaf and must perforce keep counsel."

"He would! I verily believe he would," exclaimed Grisell; "and no suspicion would light on him. How soon can I go to him, and how?"

"If it may be, this very night," said Ridley. "I missed two of the rogues, and who knows whither they may have gone?"

"Will there be time?" said the poor girl, looking round in terror.

"Certes. The nearest witch-finder is at Shields, and they cannot get there and back under two days. Have you jewels, lady? And hark you, trust not to Thora. She is the worst traitor of all. Ask me no more, but be ready to come down when you hear a whistle."

That Thora could be a traitress and turn against her - the girl whom she had taught, trained, and civilised - was too much to believe. She would almost, in spite of cautions, have asked her if it were possible, and tried to explain the true character of the services that were so cruelly misinterpreted; but as she descended the dark winding stair to supper, she heard the following colloquy:

"You will not deal hardly with her, good Ralph, dear Ralph?"

"That thou shalt see, maid! On thy life, not a word to her."

"Nay, but she is a white witch! she does no evil."

"What! Going back on what thou saidst of her brother and her mother. Take thou heed, or they will take order with thee."

"Thou wilt take care of me, good Ralph. Oh! I have done it for thee."

"Never fear, little one; only shut thy pretty little mouth;" and there was a sound of kissing.

"What will they do to her?" in a lower voice.

"Thou wilt see! Sink or swim thou knowst. Ha! ha! She will have enough of the draught that is so free to us."

Grisell, trembling and horror-stricken, could only lean against the wall hoping that her beating heart did not sound loud enough to betray her, till a call from the hall put an end to the terrible whispers.

She hurried upwards lest Thora should come up and perceive how near she had been, then descended and took her seat at supper, trying to converse with Pierce as usual, but noting with terror the absence of the two soldiers.

How her evasion was to be effected she knew not. The castle keys were never delivered to her, but always to Hardcastle, and she saw him take them; but she received from Ridley a look and sign which meant that she was to be ready, and when she left the hall she made up a bundle of needments, and in it her precious books and all the jewels she had inherited. That Thora did not follow her was a boon.

CHAPTER XIX

A MARCH HARE

Yonder is a man in sight -
Yonder is a house - but where?
No. she must not enter there.
To the caves, and to the brooks,
To the clouds of heaven she looks.

WORDSWORTH, Feast of Brougham Castle.

Long, long did Grisell kneel in an agony of prayer and terror, as she seemed already to feel savage hands putting her to the ordeal.

The castle had long been quiet and dark, so far as she knew, when there was a faint sound and a low whistle. She sprang to the door and held Ridley's hand.

"Now is the time," he said, under his breath; "the squire waits. That treacherous little baggage is safe locked into the cellar, whither I lured her to find some malvoisie for the rascaille crew. Come."

He was without his boots, and silently led the way along the narrow passage to the postern door, where stood young Hardcastle with the keys. He let them out and crossed the court with them to the little door leading to a steep descent of the cliffs by a narrow path. Not till the sands were reached did any of the three dare to speak, and then Grisell held out her hands in thanks and farewell.

"May I not guard you on your way, lady?" said Pierce.

"Best not, sir," returned Ridley; "best not know whither she is gone. I shall be back again before I am missed or your rogues are stirring."

"When Sir Leonard knows of their devices, lady," said Pierce, "then will Ridley tell him where to find you and bring you back in all honour."

Grisell could only sigh, and try to speak her thanks to the young man, who kissed her hand, and stood watching her and Ridley as the waning moon lighted them over the glistening sands, till they sought the friendly shadows of the cliffs. And thus Grisell Dacre parted from the home of her fathers.

"Cuthbert," she said, "should you see Sir Leonard, let him know that if - if he would be free from any bond to me I will aid in breaking it, and ask only dowry enough to obtain entrance to a convent, while he weds the lady he loves."

Ridley interrupted her with imprecations on the knight, and exhortations to her to hold her own, and not abandon her rights. "If he keep the lands, he should keep the wife," was his cry.

"His word and heart - " began Grisell.

"Folly, my wench. No question but she is bestowed on

some one else. You do not want to be quit of him and be mewed in a nunnery."

"I only crave to hide my head and not be the bane of his life."

"Pshaw! You have seen for yourself. Once get over the first glance and you are worth the fairest dame that ever was jousted for in the lists. Send him at least a message as though it were not your will to cast him off."

"If you will have it so, then," said Grisell, "tell him that if it be his desire, I will strive to make him a true, loyal, and loving wife."

The last words came with a sob, and Ridley gave a little inward chuckle, as of one who suspected that the duties of the good and loving wife would not be unwillingly undertaken.

Castle-bred ladies were not much given to long walks, and though the distance was only two miles, it was a good deal for Grisell, and she plodded on wearily, to the sound of the lap of the sea and the cries of the gulls. The caverns of the rock looked very black and gloomy, and she clung to Ridley, almost expecting something to spring out on her; but all was still, and the pale eastward light began to be seen over the sea before they turned away from it to ascend to the scattered houses of the little rising town.

The bells of the convent had begun to ring for lauds, but it was only twilight when they reached the wall of Lambert's garden of herbs, where there was a little door that yielded to Ridley's push. The house was still closed, and hoar frost lay on the leaves, but Grisell proposed to hide herself in the little shed which served the purpose of tool-house and summer-house till she could make her entrance. She felt sure of a welcome, and almost constrained Cuthbert to leave her, so as to return to the Tower early enough to avert suspicion - an easier matter as the men-at-arms were given to sleeping as late as they could. He would make an errand to the Apothecary's as soon as he could, so as to bring intelligence.

There sat Grisell, looking out on the brightening sky, while the blackbirds and thrushes were bursting into song, and sweet odours rising from the spring buds of the aromatic plants around, and a morning bell rang from the great monastery church. With that she saw the house door open, and Master Lambert in a fur cap and gown turned up with lambs'-wool come out into the garden, basket in hand, and chirp to the birds to come down and be fed.

It was pretty to see how the mavis and the merle, the sparrow, chaffinch, robin, and tit fluttered round, and Grisell waited a moment to watch them before she stepped forth and said, "Ah! Master Groot, here is another poor bird to implore your bounty."

"Lady Grisell," he cried, with a start.

"Ah! not that name," she said; "not a word. O Master Lambert, I came by night; none have seen me, none but good Cuthbert Ridley ken where I am. There can be no peril to you or yours if you will give shelter for a little while to a poor maid."

"Dear lady, we will do all we can," returned Lambert.

"Fear not. How pale you are. You have walked all night! Come and rest. None will follow. You are sore spent! Clemence shall bring you a warm drink! Condescend, dear lady," and he made her lean on his arm, and brought her into his large living room, and placed her in the comfortable cross-legged chair with straps and cushions as a back, while he went into some back settlement to inform his wife of her visitor; and presently they brought her warm water, with some refreshing perfume, in a brass basin, and he knelt on one knee to hold it to her, while she bathed her face and hands with a sponge - a rare luxury. She started at every sound, but Lambert assured her that she was safe, as no one ever came beyond the booth. His Clemence had no gossips, and the garden could not be overlooked. While some broth was heated for her she began to explain her peril, but he exclaimed, "Methinks I know, lady, if it was thereanent that a great strapping Hollander fellow from your Tower came to ask me for a charm against gramarie, with hints that 'twas in high places. 'Twas enough to make one laugh to see the big lubber try to whisper hints, and shiver and shake, as he showed me a knot in his matted locks and asked if it were not the enemy's tying. I told him 'twas tied by the enemy indeed, the deadly sin of sloth, and that a stout Dutchman ought to be ashamed of himself for carrying such a head within or without. But I scarce bethought me the impudent Schelm could have thought of you, lady."

"Hush again. Forget the word! They are gone to Shields in search of the witch-finder, to pinch me, and probe me, and drown me, or burn me," cried Grisell, clasping her hands. "Oh! take me somewhere if you cannot safely hide me; I would not bring trouble on you!"

"You need not fear," he answered. "None will enter here but by my goodwill, and I will bar the garden door lest any idle lad should pry in; but they come not here. The tortoise who crawls about in the summer fills them with too much terror for them to venture, and is better than any watch-dog. Now, let me touch your pulse. Ah! I would prescribe lying down on the bed and resting for the day."

She complied, and Clemence took her to the upper floor, where it was the pride of the Flemish housewife to keep a guest-chamber, absolutely neat, though very little furnished, and indeed seldom or never used; but she solicitously stroked the big bed, and signed to Grisell to lie down in the midst of pillows of down, above and below, taking off her hood, mantle, and shoes, and smoothing her down with nods and sweet smiles, so that she fell sound asleep.

When she awoke the sun was at the meridian, and she came down to the noontide meal. Master Groot was looking much entertained.

Wearmouth, he said, was in a commotion. The great Dutch Whitburn man-at-arms had come in full of the wonderful story. Not only had the grisly lady vanished, but a cross-bow man had shot an enormous hare on the moor, a creature with one ear torn off, and a seam on its face, and Masters Hardcastle and Ridley altogether favoured the belief that it was the sorceress herself without time to change her shape. Did Mynheer Groot hold with them?

For though Dutch and Flemings were not wholly friendly at home, yet in a strange country they held together, and remembered that they were both

Netherlanders, and Hannekin would fain know what thought the wise man.

"Depend on it, there was no time for a change," gravely said Groot. "Have not Nostradamus, Albertus Magnus, and Rogerus Bacon" (he was heaping names together as he saw Hannekin's big gray eyes grow rounder and rounder) "all averred that the great Diabolus can give his minions power to change themselves at will into hares, cats, or toads to transport themselves to the Sabbath on Walpurgs' night?"

"You deem it in sooth," said the Dutchman, "for know you that the parish priest swears, and so do the more part of the villein fisher folk, that there's no sorcery in the matter, but that she is a true and holy maid, with no powers save what the Saints had given her, and that her cures were by skill. Yet such was scarce like to a mere Jungvrow."

It went sorely against Master Lambert's feelings, as well as somewhat against his conscience, to encourage the notion of the death of his guest as a hare, though it ensured her safety and prevented a search. He replied that her skill certainly was uncommon in a Jungvrow, beyond nature, no doubt, and if they were unholy, it was well that the arblaster had made a riddance of her.

"By the same token," added Hannekin, "the elf lock came out of my hair this very morn, I having, as you bade me, combed it each morn with the horse's currycomb."

Proof positive, as Lambert was glad to allow him to believe. And the next day all Sunderland and the two Wearmouths believed that the dead hare had shrieked in a human voice on being thrown on a fire, and had actually shown the hands and feet of a woman before it was consumed.

It was all the safer for Grisell as long as she was not recognised, and of this there was little danger. She was scarcely known in Wearmouth, and could go to mass at the Abbey Church in a deep black hood and veil. Master Lambert sometimes received pilgrims from his own country on their way to English shrines, and she could easily pass for one of these if her presence were perceived, but except to mass in very early morning, she never went beyond the garden, where the spring beauty was enjoyment to her in the midst of her loneliness and entire doubt as to her future.

It was a grand old church, too, with low-browed arches, reminding her of the dear old chapel of Wilton, and with a lofty though undecorated square tower, entered by an archway adorned with curious twisted snakes with long beaks, stretching over and under one another.

The low heavy columns, the round circles, and the small windows, casting a very dim religious light, gave Grisell a sense of being in the atmosphere of that best beloved place, Wilton Abbey. She longed after Sister Avice's wisdom and tenderness, and wondered whether her lands would purchase from her knight, power to return thither with dower enough to satisfy the demands of the Proctor. It was a hope that seemed like an inlet of light in her loneliness, when no one was faithful save Cuthbert Ridley, and she felt cut to the heart above all by Thora's defection and cruel accusations, not knowing that half was owning to the intoxication of love, and the other half to a gossiping tongue.

Charlotte M. Yonge

CHAPTER XX

A BLIGHT ON THE WHITE ROSE

Witness Aire's unhappy water
Where the ruthless Clifford fell,
And when Wharfe ran red with slaughter
On the day of Towton's field.
Gathering in its guilty flood
The carnage and the ill spilt blood
That forty thousand lives could yield.

SOUTHEY, Funeral Song of Princess Charlotte.

Grisell from the first took her part in the Apothecary's household. Occupation was a boon to her, and she not only spun and made lace with Clemence, but showed her new patterns learned in old days at Wilton; and still more did she enjoy assisting the master of the house in making his compounds, learning new nostrums herself, and imparting others to him, showing a delicacy of finger which the old Fleming could not emulate. In the fabrication of perfumes for the pouncet box, and sweetmeats prepared with honey and sugar, she proved to have a dainty hand, so that Lambert, who would not touch her jewels, declared that she was fully earning her maintenance by the assistance that she gave to him.

They were not molested by the war, which was

decidedly a war of battles, not of sieges, but they heard far more of tidings than were wont to reach Whitburn Tower. They knew of the advance of Edward to London; and the terrible battle of Towton begun, was fought out while the snow fell far from bloodless, on Palm Sunday; and while the choir boys had been singing their Gloria, laus et honor in the gallery over the church door, shivering a little at the untimely blast, there had been grim and awful work, when for miles around the Wharfe and Aire the snow lay mixed with blood. That the Yorkists had gained was known, and that the Queen and Prince had fled; but nothing was heard of the fate of individuals, and Master Lambert was much occupied with tidings from Bruges, whence information came, in a messenger sent by a notary that his uncle, an old miser, whose harsh displeasure at his marriage had driven him forth, was just dead, leaving him heir to a fairly prosperous business and a house in the city.

To return thither was of course Lambert's intention as soon as he could dispose of his English property. He entreated Grisell to accompany him and Clemence, assuming her that at the chief city of so great a prince as Duke Philip of Burgundy, she would have a better hope of hearing tidings of her husband than in a remote town like Sunderland; and that if she still wished to dispose of her jewels she would have a far better chance of so doing. He was arguing the point with her, when there was a voice in the stall outside which made Grisell start, and Lambert, going out, brought in Cuthbert Ridley, staggering under the weight of his best suit of armour, and with a bundle and bag under his mantle.

Grisell sprang up eagerly to meet him, but as she put

her hands into his he looked sorrowfully at her, and she asked under her breath, "Ah! Sir Leonard - ?"

"No tidings of the recreant," growled Ridley, "but ill tidings for both of you. The Dacres of Gilsland are on us, claiming your castle and lands as male heirs to your father."

"Do they know that I live?" asked Grisell, "or" - unable to control a little laugh - "do they deem that I was slain in the shape of a hare?"

"Or better than that," put in Lambert; "they have it now in the wharves that the corpse of the hare took the shape and hands of a woman when in the hall."

"I ken not, the long-tongued rogues," said Ridley; "but if my young lady were standing living and life-like before them as, thank St. Hilda, I see her now, they would claim it all the more as male heirs, and this new King Edward has granted old Sir John seisin, being that she is the wife of one of King Henry's men!"

"Are they there? How did you escape?"

"I got timely notice," said Cuthbert. "Twenty strong halted over the night at Yeoman Kester's farm on Heather Gill - a fellow that would do anything for me since we fought side by side on the day of the Herrings. So he sends out his two grandsons to tell me what they were after, while they were drinking his good ale to health of their King Edward. So forewarned, forearmed. We have left them empty walls, get in as they can or may - unless that traitor Tordu chooses to stay and make terms with them."

"Master Hardcastle! Would he fly? Surely not!" asked Grisell.

"Master Hardcastle, with Dutch Hannekin and some of the better sort, went off long since to join their knight's banner, and the Saints know how the poor young lad sped in all the bloody work they have had. For my part, I felt not bound to hold out the castle against my old lord's side, when there was no saving it for you, so I put what belonged to me together, and took poor old Roan, and my young lady's pony, and made my way hither, no one letting me. I doubt me much, lady, that there is little hope of winning back your lands, whatever side may be uppermost, yet there be true hearts among our villeins, who say they will never pay dues to any save their lord's daughter."

"Then I am landless and homeless," sighed Grisell.

"The greater cause that you should make your home with us, lady," returned Lambert Groot; and he went on to lay before Ridley the state of the case, and his own plans. House and business, possibly a seat in the city council, were waiting for him at Bruges, and the vessel from Ostend which had continually brought him supplies for his traffic was daily expected. He intended, so soon as she had made up her cargo of wool, to return in her to his native country, and he was urgent that the Lady Grisell should go with him, representing that all the changes of fortune in the convulsed kingdom of England were sure to be quickly known there, and that she was as near the centre of action in Flanders as in Durham, besides that she would be out of reach of any enemies who might disbelieve the hare transformation.

After learning the fate of her castle, Grisell much inclined to the proposal which kept her with those whom she had learnt to trust and love, and she knew that she need be no burthen to them, since she had profitable skill in their own craft, and besides she had her jewels. Ridley, moreover, gave her hopes of a certain portion of her dues on the herring-boats and the wool.

"Will not you come with the lady, sir?" asked Lambert.

"Oh, come!" cried Grisell.

"Nay, a squire of dames hath scarce been heard of in a Poticar's shop," said Ridley, and there was an irresistible laugh at the rugged old gentleman so terming himself; but as Lambert and Grisell were both about to speak he went on, "I can serve her better elsewhere. I am going first to my home at Willimoteswick. I have not seen it these forty year, and whether my brother or my nephew make me welcome or no, I shall have seen the old moors and mosses. Then methought I would come hither, or to some of the towns about, and see how it fares with the old Tower and the folk; and if they be as good as their word, and keep their dues for my lady, I could gather them, and take or bring them to her, with any other matter which might concern her nearly."

This was thoroughly approved by Grisell's little council, and Lambert undertook to make known to the good esquire the best means of communication, whether in person, or by the transmission of payments, since all the eastern ports of England had connections with Dutch and Flemish traffic, which made the payment of monies possible.

Grisell meantime was asking for Thora. Her uncle, Ridley said, had come up, laid hands on her, and soundly scourged her for her foul practices. He had dragged her home, and when Ralph Hart had come after her, had threatened him with a quarter-staff, called out a mob of fishermen, and finally had brought him to Sir Lucas, who married them willy-nilly. He was the runaway son of a currier in York, and had taken her en croupe, and ridden off to his parents at the sign of the Hart, to bespeak their favour.

Grisell grieved deeply over Thora's ingratitude to her, and the two elder men foreboded no favourable reception for the pair, and hoped that Thora would sup sorrow.

Ridley spent the night at the sign of tire Green Serpent, and before he set out for Willimoteswick, he confided to Master Groot a bag containing a silver cup or two, and a variety of coins, mostly French. They were, he said, spoils of his wars under King Harry the Fifth and the two Lord Salisburys, which he had never had occasion to spend, and he desired that they might be laid out on the Lady Grisell in case of need, leaving her to think they were the dues from her faithful tenantry. To the Hausvrow Clemence it was a great grief to leave the peaceful home of her married life, and go among kindred who had shown their scorn in neglect and cold looks; but she kept a cheerful face for her husband, and only shed tears over the budding roses and other plants she had to leave; and she made her guest understand how great a comfort and solace was her company.

CHAPTER XXI

THE WOUNDED KNIGHT

Belted Will Howard is marching here,
And hot Lord Dacre with many a spear

SCOTT, The Lay of the Last Minstrel.

"Master Groot, a word with you." A lay brother in the coarse, dark robe of St. Benedict was standing in the booth of the Green Serpent.

Groot knew him for Brother Christopher of Monks Wearmouth, and touched his brow in recognition.

"Have you here any balsam fit for a plaguey shot with an arquebuss, the like of which our poor peaceful house never looked to harbour?"

"For whom is it needed, good brother?"

"Best not ask," said Brother Christopher, who was, however, an inveterate gossip, and went on in reply to Lambert's question as to the place of the wound. "In the shoulder is the worst, the bullet wound where the Brother Infirmarer has poured in hot oil. St. Bede! How the poor knight howled, though he tried to stop it, and brought it down to moaning. His leg is broken beside, but we could deal with that. His horse went down with him, you see, when he was overtaken and shot down by the Gilsland folk."

"The Gilsland folk!"

"Even so, poor lad; and he was only on his way to see after his own, or his wife's, since all the Whitburn sons are at an end, and the Tower gone to the spindle side. They say, too, that the damsel he wedded perforce was given to magic, and fled in form of a hare. But be that as it will, young Copeland - St. Bede, pardon me! What have I let out?"

"Reck not of that, brother. The tale is all over the town. How of Copeland?"

"As I said even now, he was on his way to the Tower, when the Dacres-Will and Harry - fell on him, and left him for dead; but by the Saints' good providence, his squire and groom put him on a horse, and brought him to our Abbey at night, knowing that he is kin to our Sub-Prior. And there he lies, whether for life or death only Heaven knows, but for death it will be if only King Edward gets a scent of him; so hold your peace, Master Groats, as to who it be, as you live, or as you would not have his blood on you."

Master Groats promised silence, and gave numerous directions as to the application of his medicaments, and Brother Kit took his leave, reiterating assurances that Sir Leonard's life depended on his secrecy.

Whatever was said in the booth was plainly audible in the inner room. Grisell and Clemence were packing linen, and the little shutter of the wooden partition was open. Thus Lambert found Grisell standing with clasped hands, and a face of intense attention and suspense.

"You have heard, lady," he said.

"Oh, yea, yea! Alas, poor Leonard!" she cried.

"The Saints grant him recovery."

"Methought you would be glad to hear you were like to be free from such a yoke. Were you rid of him, you, of a Yorkist house, might win back your lands, above all, since, as you once told me, you were a playmate of the King's sister."

"Ah! dear master, speak not so! Think of him! treacherously wounded, and lying moaning. That gruesome oil! Oh! my poor Leonard!" and she burst into tears. "So fair, and comely, and young, thus stricken down!"

"Bah!" exclaimed Lambert. "Such are women! One would think she loved him, who flouted her!"

"I cannot brook the thought of his lying there in sore pain and dolour, he who has had so sad a life, baulked of his true love."

Master Lambert could only hold up his hands at the perversity of womankind, and declare to his Clemence that he verily believed that had the knight been a true and devoted Tristram himself, ever at her feet, the lady could not have been so sore troubled.

The next day brought Brother Kit back with an earnest

request from the Infirmarer and the Sub-Prior that "Master Groats" would come to the monastery, and give them the benefit of his advice on the wounds and the fever which was setting in, since gun-shot wounds were beyond the scope of the monastic surgery.

To refuse would not have been possible, even without the earnest entreaty of Grisell; and Lambert, who had that medical instinct which no training can supply, went on his way with the lay brother.

He came back after many hours, sorely perturbed by the request that had been made to him. Sir Leonard, he said, was indeed sick nigh unto death, grievously hurt, and distraught by the fever, or it might be by the blow on his head in the fall with his horse, which seemed to have kicked him; but there was no reason that with good guidance and rest he should not recover. But, on the other hand, King Edward was known to be on his progress to Durham, and he was understood to be especially virulent against Sir Leonard Copeland, under the impression that the young knight had assisted in Clifford's slaughter of his brother Edmund of Rutland. It was true that a monastery was a sanctuary, but if all that was reported of Edward Plantagenet were true, he might, if he tracked Copeland to the Abbey, insist on his being yielded up, or might make Abbot and monks suffer severely for the protection given to his enemy; and there was much fear that the Dacres might be on the scent. The Abbot and Father Copeland were anxious to be able to answer that Sir Leonard was not within their precincts, and, having heard that Master Groats was about to sail for Flanders, the Sub-Prior made the entreaty that his nephew might thus be conveyed to the Low Countries, where the fugitives of each party in turn found a refuge. Father Copeland promised to be at charges, and, in truth, the scheme was the best hope for Leonard's chances of life. Master Groot had hesitated, seeing various difficulties in the way of such a charge, and being by no means disposed towards Lady Grisell's unwilling husband, as such, though in a professional capacity he was interested in his treatment of his patient, and was likewise touched by the good mien of the fine, handsome, straight-limbed young man, who was lying unconscious on his pallet in a narrow cell.

He had replied that he would answer the next day, when he had consulted his wife and the ship-master, whose consent was needful; and there was of course another, whom he did not mention.

As he told all the colour rose in Grisell's face, rosy on one side, purple, alas, on the other. "O master, good master, you will, you will!"

"Is it your pleasure, then, mistress? I should have held that the kindness to you would be to rid you of him."

"No, no, no! You are mocking me! You know too well what I think! Is not this my best hope of making him know me, and becoming his true and - and -"

A sob cut her short, but she cried, "I will be at all the pains and all the cost, if only you will consent, dear Master Lambert, good Master Groot."

"Ah, would I knew what is well for her!" said Lambert, turning to his wife, and making rapid signs with face and fingers in their mutual language, but Grisell burst in -

"Good for her," cried she. "Can it be good for a wife to leave her husband to be slain by the cruel men of York and Warwick, him who strove to save the young Lord Edmund? Master, you will suffer no such foul wrong. O master, if you did, I would stay behind, in some poor hovel on the shore, where none would track him, and tend him there. I will! I vow it to St. Mary."

"Hush, hush, lady! Cease this strange passion. You could not be more moved if he were the tenderest spouse who ever breathed."

"But you will have pity, sir. You will aid us. You will save us. Give him the chance for life."

"What say you, housewife?" said Groot, turning to the silent Clemence, whom his signs and their looks had made to perceive the point at issue. Her reply was to seize Grisell's two hands, kiss them fervently, clasp both together, and utter in her deaf voice two Flemish words, "Goot Vrow." Grisell eagerly embraced her in tears.

"We have still to see what Skipper Vrowst says. He may not choose to meddle with English outlaws."

"If you cannot win him to take my knight, he will not take me," said Grisell.

There was no more to be said except something about the waywardness of the affections of women and dogs; but Master Groot was not ill-pleased at the bottom that both the females of the household took part against him, and they had a merry supper that night, amid the chests in which their domestic apparatus and stock-in-trade were packed, with the dried lizard, who passed for a crocodile, sitting on the settle as if he were one of the company. Grisell's spirits rose with an undefined hope that, like Sir Gawaine's bride, or her own namesake, Griselda the patient, she should at last win her lord's love; and, deprived as she was of all her own relatives, there arose strongly within her the affection that ten long years ago had made her haunt the footsteps of the boy at Amesbury Manor.

Groot was made to promise to say not a word of her presence in his family. He was out all day, while Clemence worked hard at her demenagement, and only with scruples accepted the assistance of her guest, who was glad to work away her anxiety in the folding of curtains and stuffing of mails.

At last Lambert returned, having been backwards and forwards many times between the Vrow Gudule and the Abbey, for Skipper Vrowst drove a hard bargain, and made the most of the inconvenience and danger of getting into ill odour with the authorities; and, however anxious Father Copeland might be to save his nephew, Abbot and bursar demurred at gratifying extortion, above all when the King might at any time be squeezing them for contributions hard to come by.

However, it had been finally fixed that a boat should put in to the Abbey steps to receive the fleeces of the sheep-shearing of the home grange, and that, rolled in one of these fleeces, the wounded knight should be brought on board the Vrow Gudule, where Groot and the women would await him, their freight being already embarked, and all ready to weigh anchor.

The chief danger was in a King's officer coming on board to weigh the fleeces, and obtaining the toll on them. But Sunderland either had no King, or had two just at that time, and Father Copeland handed Master Groot a sum which might bribe one or both; while it was to the interest of the captain to make off without being overhauled by either.

Charlotte M. Yonge

CHAPTER XXII

THE CITY OF BRIDGES

So for long hours sat Enid by her lord,
There in the naked hall, propping his head,
And chafing his pale hands, and calling to him.
And at the last he waken'd from his swoon.

TENNYSON, Enid.

The transit was happily effected, and closely hidden in
wool, Leonard Copeland was lifted out the boat, more
than half unconscious, and afterwards transferred to
the vessel, and placed in wrappings as softly and
securely as Grisell and Clemence could arrange before
King Edward's men came to exact their poundage on
the freight, but happily did not concern themselves
about the sick man.

He might almost be congratulated on his semi-
insensibility, for though he suffered, he would not
retain the recollection of his suffering, and the voyage
was very miserable to every one, though the weather
was far from unfavourable, as the captain declared.
Grisell indeed was so entirely taken up with
ministering to her knight that she seemed impervious
to sickness or discomfort. It was a great relief to enter
on the smooth waters of the great canal from Ostend,

and Lambert stood on the deck recognising old landmarks, and pointing them out with the joy of homecoming to Clemence, who perhaps felt less delight, since the joys of her life had only begun when she turned her back on her unkind kinsfolk.

Nor did her face light up as his did while he pointed out to Grisell the beauteous belfry, rising on high above the many-peaked gables, though she did smile when a long-billed, long-legged stork flapped his wings overhead, and her husband signed that it was in greeting. The greeting that delighted him she could not hear, the sweet chimes from that same tower, which floated down the stream, when he doffed his cap, crossed himself, and clasped his hands in devout thanksgiving.

It was a wonderful scene of bustle; where vessels of all kinds thronged together were drawn up to the wharf, the beautiful tall painted ships of Venice and Genoa pre-eminent among the stoutly-built Netherlanders and the English traders. Shouts in all languages were heard, and Grisell looked round in wonder and bewilderment as to how the helpless and precious charge on the deck was ever to be safely landed.

Lambert, however, was truly at home and equal to the occasion. He secured some of the men who came round the vessel in barges clamouring for employment, and - Grisell scarce knew how - Leonard on his bed was lifted down, and laid in the bottom of the barge. The big bundles and cases were committed to the care of another barge, to follow close after theirs, and on they went under, one after another, the numerous high-peaked bridges to which Bruges owes its name, while tall sharp-gabled houses, walls, or sometimes pleasant green gardens, bounded the margins, with a narrow foot-way between. The houses had often pavement leading by stone steps to the river, and stone steps up to the door, which was under the deep projecting eaves running along the front of the house - a stoop, as the Low Countries called it. At one of these - not one of the largest or handsomest, but far superior to the old home at Sunderland - hung the large handsome painted and gilded sign of the same serpent which Grisell had learnt to know so well, and here the barge hove to, while two servants, the man in a brown belted jerkin, the old woman in a narrow, tight, white hood, came out on the steps with outstretched hands.

"Mein Herr, my dear Master Lambert. Oh, joy! Greet thee well. Thanks to our Lady that I have lived to see this day," was the old woman's cry.

"Greet thee well, dear old Mother Abra. Greet thee, trusty Anton. You had my message? Have you a bed and chamber ready for this gentleman?"

Such was Lambert's hasty though still cordial greeting, as he gave his hand to the man-servant, his cheek to his old nurse, who was mother to Anton. Clemence in her gentle dumb show shared the welcome, and directed as Leonard was carried up an outside stone stair to a guest-chamber, and deposited in a stately bed with fresh, cool, lace-bordered, lavender-scented sheets, and Grisell put between his lips a spoonful of the cordial with which Lambert had supplied her.

More distinctly than before he murmured, "Thanks, sweet Eleanor."

The move in the open air had partly revived him, partly

made him feverish, and he continued to murmur complacently his thanks to Eleanor for tending her "wounded knight," little knowing whom he wounded by his thanks.

On one point this decided Grisell. She looked up at Lambert, and when he used her title of "Lady," in begging her to leave old Mother Abra in charge and to come down to supper, she made a gesture of silence, and as she came down the broad stair - a refinement scarce known in England - she entreated him to let her be Grisell still.

"Unless he accept me as his wife I will never bear his name," she said.

"Nay, madame, you are Lady of Whitburn by right."

"By right, may be, but not in fact, nor could I be known as mine own self without cumbering him with my claims. No, let me alone to be Grisell as ever before, an English orphan, bower-woman to Vrow Clemence if she will have me."

Clemence would not consent to treat her as bower-woman, and it was agreed that she should remain as one of the many orphans made by the civil war in England, without precise definition of her rank, and be only called by her Christian name. She was astonished at the status of Master Groot, the size and furniture of the house, and the servants who awaited him; all so unlike his little English establishment, for the refinements and even luxuries were not only far beyond those of Whitburn, but almost beyond all that she had seen even in the households of the Earls of Salisbury and Warwick. He had indeed been bred to all this, for the burghers of Bruges were some of the most prosperous of all the rich citizens of Flanders in the golden days of the Dukes of Burgundy; and he had left it all for the sake of his Clemence, but without forfeiting his place in his Guild, or his right to his inheritance.

He was, however, far from being a rich man, on a level with the great merchants, though he had succeeded to a modest, not unprosperous trade in spices, drugs, condiments and other delicacies.

He fetched a skilful Jewish physician to visit Sir Leonard Copeland, but there was no great difference in the young man's condition for many days. Grisell nursed him indefatigably, sitting by him so as to hear the sweet bells chime again and again, and the storks clatter on the roofs at sunrise.

Still, whenever her hand brought him some relief, or she held drink to his lips, his words and thanks were for Eleanor, and more and more did the sense sink down upon her like lead that she must give him up to Eleanor.

Yes, it was like lead, for, as she watched his face on the pillow her love went out to him. It might have done so even had he been disfigured like herself; but his was a beautiful countenance of noble outlines, and she felt a certain pride in it as hers, while she longed to see it light up with reason, and glow once more with health. Then she thought she could rejoice, even if there were no look of love for her.

The eyes did turn towards her again with the mind looking out of them, and he knew her for the nurse on whom he depended for comfort and relief. He thanked her courteously, so that she felt a thrill of pleasure every time. He even learnt her name of Grisell, and once he asked whether she were not English, to which she replied simply that she was, and on a further question she said that she had been at Sunderland with Master Groot, and that she had lost her home in the course of the wars.

There for some time it rested - rested at least with the knight. But with the lady there was far from rest, for every hour she was watching for some favourable token which might draw them nearer, and give opportunity for making herself known. Nearer they certainly drew, for he often smiled at her. He liked her to wait on him, and to beguile the weariness of his recovery by singing to him, telling some of her store of tales, or reading to him, for books were more plentiful at Bruges than at Sunderland, and there were even whispers of a wonderful mode of multiplying them far more quickly than by the scrivener's hand.

How her heart beat every time she thus ministered to him, or heard his voice call to her, but it was all, as she could plainly see, just as he would have spoken to Clemence, if she could have heard him, and he evidently thought her likewise of burgher quality, and much of the same age as the Vrow Groot. Indeed, the long toil and wear of the past months had made her thin and haggard, and the traces of her disaster were all the more apparent, so that no one would have guessed her years to be eighteen.

She had taken her wedding-ring from her finger, and wore it on a chain, within her kirtle, so as to excite no inquiry. But many a night, ere she lay down, she

Charlotte M. Yonge

looked at it, and even kissed it, as she asked herself whether her knight would ever bid her wear it. Until he did so her finger should never again be encircled by it.

Meantime she scarcely ever went beyond the nearest church and the garden, which amply compensated Clemence for that which she had left at Sunderland. Indeed, that had been as close an imitation of this one as Lambert could contrive in a colder climate with smaller means. Here was a fountain trellised over by a framework rich in roses and our lady's bower; here were pinks, gilly-flowers, pansies, lavender, and the new snowball shrub recently produced at Gueldres, and a little bush shown with great pride by Anton, the snow-white rose grown in King Rene's garden of Provence.

These served as borders to the green walks dividing the beds of useful vegetables and fruits and aromatic herbs which the Groots had long been in the habit of collecting from all parts and experimenting on. Much did Lambert rejoice to find himself among the familiar plants he had often needed and could not procure in England, and for some of which he had a real individual love. The big improved distillery and all the jars and bottles of his youth were a joy to him, almost as much as the old friends who accepted him again after a long "wander year."

Clemence had her place too, but she shrank from the society she could not share, and while most of the burghers' wives spent the summer evening sitting spinning or knitting on the steps of the stoop, conversing with their gossips, she preferred to take her distaff or needle among the roses, sometimes tending them, sometimes beguiling Grisell to come and take the air in company with her, for they understood one another's mute language; and when Lambert Groot was with his old friends they sufficed for one another - so far as Grisell's anxious heart could find solace, and perhaps in none so much as the gentle matron who could caress but could not talk.

CHAPTER XXIII

THE CANKERED OAK GALL

That Walter was no fool, though that him list
To change his wif, for it was for the best;
For she is fairer, so they demen all,
Than his Griselde, and more tendre of age.

CHAUCER, The Clerke's Tale.

It was on an early autumn evening when the belfry stood out beautiful against the sunset sky, and the storks with their young fledglings were wheeling homewards to their nest on the roof, that Leonard was lying on the deep oriel window of the guest-chamber, and Grisell sat opposite to him with a lace pillow on her lap, weaving after the pattern of Wilton for a Church vestment.

"The storks fly home," he said. "I marvel whether we have still a home in England, or ever shall have one!"

"I heard tell that the new King of France is friendly to the Queen and her son," said Grisell.

"He is near of kin to them, but he must keep terms with this old Duke who sheltered him so long. Still, when he is firm fixed on his throne he may yet bring home our brave young Prince and set the blessed King on his throne once more."

"Ah! You love the King."

"I revere him as a saint, and feel as though I drew my sword in a holy cause when I fight for him," said Leonard, raising himself with glittering eyes.

"And the Queen?"

"Queen Margaret! Ah! by my troth she is a dame who makes swords fly out of their scabbards by her brave stirring words and her noble mien. Her bright eyes and undaunted courage fire each man's heart in her cause till there is nothing he would not do or dare, ay, or give up for her, and those she loves better than herself, her husband, and her son."

"You have done so," faltered Grisell.

"Ah! have I not? Mistress, I would that you bore any other name. You mind me of the bane and grief of my life."

"Verily?" uttered Grisell with some difficulty.

"Yea! Tell me, mistress, have I ever, when my brains were astray, uttered any name?"

"By times, even so!" she confessed.

"I thought so! I deemed at times that she was here! I have never told you of the deed that marred my life."

" Nay , " she said, letting her bobbins fall though she

Charlotte M. Yonge

drooped her head, not daring to look him in the face.

"I was a mere lad, a page in the Earl of Salisbury's house. A good man was he, but the jealousies and hatreds of the nobles had begun long ago, and the good King hoped, as he ever hoped, to compose them. So he brought about a compact between my father and the Dacre of Whitburn for a marriage between their children, and caused us both to be bred up in the Lady of Salisbury's household, meaning, I trow, that we should enter into solemn contract when we were of less tender age; but there never was betrothal; and before any fit time for it had come, I had the mishap to have the maid close to me - she was ever besetting and running after me - when by some prank, unhappily of mine, a barrel of gunpowder blew up and wellnigh tore her to pieces. My father came, and her mother, an unnurtured, uncouth woman, who would have forced me to wed her on the spot, but my father would not hear of it, more especially as there were then two male heirs, so that I should not have gained her grim old Tower and bare moorlands. All held that I was not bound to her; the Queen herself owned it, and that whatever the damsel might be, the mother was a mere northern she-bear, whose child none would wish to wed, and of the White Rose besides. So the King had me to his school at Eton, and then I was a squire of my Lord of Somerset, and there I saw my fairest Eleanor Audley. The Queen and the Duke of Somerset - rest his soul - would have had us wedded. On the love day, when all walked together to St. Paul's, and the King hoped all was peace, we spoke our vows to one another in the garden of Westminster. She gave me this rook, I gave her the jewel of my cap; I read her true love in her eyes, like our limpid northern brooks. Oh! she was fair, fairer than yonder star in the sunset, but her father, the Lord Audley, was absent, and we could go no farther; and therewith came the Queen's summons to her liegemen to come and arrest Salisbury at Bloreheath. There never was rest again, as you know. My father was slain at Northampton, I yielded me to young Falconberg; but I found the Yorkists had set headsmen to work as though we had been traitors, and I was begging for a priest to hear my shrift, when who should come into the foul, wretched barn where we lay awaiting the rope, but old Dacre of Whitburn. He had craved me from the Duke of York, it seems, and gained my life on what condition he did not tell me, but he bound my feet beneath my horse, and thus bore me out of the camp for all the first day. Then, I own he let me ride as became a knight, on my word of honour not to escape; but much did I marvel whether it were revenge or ransom that he wanted; and as to ransom, all our gold had all been riding on horseback with my poor father. What he had devised I knew not nor guessed till late at night we were at his rat-hole of a Tower, where I looked for a taste of the dungeons; but no such thing. The choice that the old robber -"

Grisell could not repress a dissentient murmur of indignation.

"Ah, well, you are from Sunderland, and may know better of him. But any way the choice he left me was the halter that dangled from the roof and his grisly daughter!"

"Did you see her?" Grisell contrived to ask.

"I thank the Saints, no. To hear of her was enow. They say she has a face like a cankered oak gall or a rotten apple lying cracked on the ground among the wasps.

Mayhap though you have seen her."

Grisell could truly say, in a half-choked voice, "Never since she was a child," for no mirror had come in her way since she was at Warwick House. She was upborne by the thought that it would be a relief to him not to see anything like a rotten apple. He went on -

"My first answer and first thought was rather death - and of my word to my Eleanor. Ah! you marvel to see me here now. I felt as though nothing would make me a recreant to her. Her sweet smile and shining eyes rose up before me, and half the night I dreamt of them, and knew that I would rather die than be given to another and be false to them. Ah! but you will deem me a recreant. With the waking hours I thought of my King and Queen. My elder brother died with Lord Shrewsbury in Gascony, and after me the next heir is a devoted Yorkist who would turn my castle, the key of Cleveland, against the Queen. I knew the defeat would make faithful swords more than ever needful to her, and that it was my bounden duty, if it were possible, to save my life, my sword, and my lands for her. Mistress, you are a good woman. Did I act as a coward?"

"You offered up yourself," said Grisell, looking up.

"So it was! I gave my consent, on condition that I should be free at once. We were wedded in the gloom - ere sunrise - a thunderstorm coming up, which so darkened the church that if she had been a peerless beauty, fair as Cressid herself, I could not have seen her, and even had she been beauty itself, nought can to me be such as my Eleanor. So I was free to gallop off through the storm for Wearmouth when the rite was over, and none pursued me, for old Whitburn was a man of his word. Mine uncle held the marriage as nought, but next I made for the Queen at Durham, and, if aught could comfort my spirit, it was her thanks, and assurances that it would cost nothing but the dispensation of the Pope to set me free. So said Dr. Morton, her chaplain, one of the most learned men in England. I told him all, and he declared that no wedlock was valid without the heartfelt consent of each party."

"Said he so?" Poor Grisell could not repress the inquiry.

"Yea, and that though no actual troth had passed between me and Lord Audley's daughter, yet that the vows we had of our own free will exchanged would be quite enough to annul my forced marriage."

"You think it evil in me, the more that it was I who had defaced that countenance. I thought of that! I would have endowed her with all I had if she would set me free. I trusted yet so to do, when, for my misfortune as well as hers, the day of Wakefield cut off her father and brother, and a groom was taken who was on his way to Sendal with tidings of the other brother's death. Then, what do the Queen and Sir Pierre de Breze but command me to ride off instantly to claim Whitburn Tower! In vain did I refuse; in vain did I plead that if I were about to renounce the lady it were unknightly to seize on her inheritance. They would not hear me. They said it would serve as a door to England, and that it must be secured for the King, or the Dacres would hold it for York. They bade me on my allegiance, and commanded me to take it in King Henry's name, as though it were a mere stranger's castle, and gave me a crew of hired men-at-arms, as I verily believe to watch over what I did. But ere I started I made a vow in Dr. Morton's hands, to take it only for the King, and so soon as the troubles be ended to restore it to the lady, when our marriage is dissolved. As it fell out, I never saw the lady. Her mother lay a-dying, and there was no summoning her. I bade them show her all due honour, hoisted my pennon, rode on to my uncle at Wearmouth, and thence to mine own lands, whence I joined the Queen on her way to London. As you well know, all was over with our cause at Towton Moor; and it was on my way northward after the deadly fight that half a dozen of the men-at-arms brought me tidings, not only that the Gilsland Dacres had, as had been feared, claimed the castle, but that this same so-called lady of mine had been shown to deal in sorcery and magic. They sent for a wise man from Shields, but she found by her arts what they were doing, fled, and was slain by an arquebuss in the form of a hare!

"Do you believe it was herself in sooth?" asked Grisell.

"Ah! you are bred by Master Lambert, who, like his kind, hath little faith in sorcery, but verily, old women do change into hares. All have known them."

"She was scarce old," Grisell trusted herself to say.

"That skills not. They said she made strange cures by no rules of art. Ay, and said her prayers backward, and had unknown books."

"Did your squire tell this, or was it only the men?"

"My squire! Poor Pierce, I never saw him. He was made captive by a White Rose party, so far as I could hear, and St. Peter knows where he may be. But look you, the lady, for all her foul looks, had cast her spell over him, and held him as bound and entranced as by a true love, so that he was ready to defend her beauty - her beauty! Look you! - against all the world in the lists. He was neither to have nor to hold if any man durst utter a word against her! And it was the same with her tirewoman and her own old squire."

"Then, sir, you deem that in slaying the hare, the arquebusier rid you of your witch wife?" There was a little bitterness, even scorn, in the tone.

"I say not so, mistress. I know men-at-arms too well to credit all they say, and I was on my way to inquire into the matter and learn the truth when these same Dacres fell on me; and that I lie here is due to you and good Master Lambert. Many a woman whose face is ill favoured has learnt to keep up her power by unhallowed arts, and if it be so with her whom in my boyish prank I have marred, Heaven forgive her and me. If I can ever return I shall strive to trace her life or death, without which mayhap I could scarce win my true bride."

Grisell could bear no more of this crushing of her hopes. She crept away murmuring something about the vesper bell at the convent chapel near, for it was there that she could best kneel, while thoughts and strength and resolution came to her.

The one thing clear to her was that Sir Leonard did not view her, or rather the creature at Whitburn Tower, as his wife, but as a hag, mayhap a sorceress from whom he desired to be released, and that his love to Eleanor Audley was as strong as ever.

Should she make herself known and set him free? Nay, but then what would become of him? He still needed her care, which he accepted as that of a nurse, and while he believed himself to be living on the means supplied by his uncle at Wearmouth to the Apothecary, this had soon been exhausted, and Grisell had partly supplied what was wanting from Ridley's bag, partly from what the old squire had sent her as the fishermen's dues; and she was perceiving how to supplement this, or replace it by her own skill, by her assistance to Lambert in his concoctions, and likewise by her lace-work, which was of a device learnt at Wilton and not known at Bruges. There was something strangely delightful to her in thus supporting Leonard even though he knew it not, and she determined to persist in her present course till there was some change. Suppose he heard of Eleanor's marriage to some one else! Then? But, ah, the cracked apple face. She must find a glass, or even a pail of water, and judge! Or the Lancastrian fortunes might revive, he might go home in triumph, and then would she give him her ring and her renunciation, and either earn enough to obtain entrance to a convent or perhaps be accepted for the sake of her handiwork!

Any way the prospect was dreary, and the affection which grew upon her as Leonard recovered only made it sadder. To reveal herself would only be misery to him, and in his present state of mind would deprive him of all he needed, since he would never be base enough to let her toil for him and then cast her off.

She thought it best, or rather she yearned so much for counsel, that at night, over the fire in the stove, she told what Leonard had said, to which her host listened with the fatherly sympathy that had grown up towards her. He was quite determined against her making herself known. The accusation of sorcery really alarmed him. He said that to be known as the fugitive heiress of Whitburn who had bewitched the young squire and many more might bring both her and himself into imminent danger; and there were Lancastrian exiles who might take up the report. Her only safety was in being known, to the few who did meet her, as the convent-bred maiden whose home had been destroyed, and who was content to gain a livelihood as the assistant whom his wife's infirmity made needful. As to Sir Leonard, the knight's own grace and gratitude had endeared him, as well as the professional pleasure of curing him, and for the lady's sake he should still be made welcome.

So matters subsided. No one knew Grisell's story except Master Lambert and her Father Confessor, and whether he really knew it, through the medium of her imperfect French, might be doubted. Even Clemence, though of course aware of her identity, did not know all the details, since no one who could communicate with her had thought it well to distress her with the witchcraft story.

Few came beyond the open booth, which served as shop, though sometimes there would be admitted to walk in the garden and converse with Master Groot, a young Englishman who wanted his counsel on giving permanence and clearness to the ink he was using in that newart of printing which he was trying to perfect, but which there were some who averred to be a work of the Evil One, imparted to the magician Dr. Faustus.

CHAPTER XXIV

GRISELL'S PATIENCE

When silent were both voice and chords,
The strain seemed doubly dear,
Yet sad as sweet, - for English words
Had fallen upon the ear.

WORDSWORTH, Incident at Bruges.

Meanwhile Leonard was recovering and vexing himself as to his future course, inclining chiefly to making his way back to Wearmouth to ascertain how matters were going in England.

One afternoon, however, as he sat close to thine window, while Grisell sang to him one of her sweet old ballads, a face, attracted by the English words and voice, was turned up to him. He exclaimed, "By St. Mary, Philip Scrope," and starting up, began to feel for the stick which he still needed.

A voice was almost at the same moment heard from the outer shop inquiring in halting French, "Did I see the face of the Beau Sire Leonard Copeland?"

By the time Leonard had hobbled to the door into the booth, a tall perfectly-equipped man-at-arms, in velvet bonnet with the Burgundian Cross, bright cuirass, rich crimson surcoat, and handsome sword belt, had advanced, and the two embraced as old friends did embrace in the middle ages, especially when each had believed the other dead.

"I deemed thee dead at Towton!"

"Methought you were slain in the north! You have not come off scot-free."

"Nay, but I had a narrow escape. My honest fellows took me to my uncle at Wearmouth, and he shipped me off with the good folk here, and cares for my maintenance. How didst thou 'scape?"

"Half a dozen of us - Will Percy and a few more - made off from the woful field under cover of night, and got to the sea-shore, to a village - I know not the name - and laid hands on a fisher's smack, which Jock of Hull was seaman enough to steer with the aid of the lad on board, as far as Friesland, and thence we made our way as best we could to Utrecht, where we had the luck to fall in with one of the Duke's captains, who was glad enough to meet with a few stout fellows to make up his company of men-at-arms."

"Oh! Methought it was the Cross of Burgundy. How art thou so well attired, Phil?"

"We have all been pranked out to guard our Duke to the King of France's sacring at Rheims. I promise thee the jewels and gold blazed as we never saw the like - and as to the rascaille Scots archers, every one of them was arrayed so as the sight was enough to drive an honest Borderer crazy. Half their own kingdom's worth

Charlotte M. Yonge

was on their beggarly backs. But do what they might, our Duke surpassed them all with his largesses and splendour."

"Your Duke!" grumbled Leonard.

"Aye, mine for the nonce, and a right open-handed lord is he. Better be under him than under the shrivelled skinflint of France, who wore his fine robes as though they galled him. Come and take service here when thou art whole of thine hurt, Leonard."

"I thought thy Duke was disinclined to Lancaster."

"He may be to the Queen and the poor King, whom the Saints guard, but he likes English hearts and thews in his pay well enough."

"Thou knowst I am a knight, worse luck."

"Heed not for thy knighthood. The Duke of Exeter and my Lord of Oxford have put their honours in their pouch and are serving him. Thy lame leg is a worse hindrance than the gold spur on it, but I trow that will pass."

The comrades talked on, over the fate of English friends and homes, and the hopelessness of their cause. It was agreed in this, and in many subsequent visits from Scrope, that so soon as Leonard should have shaken off his lameness he should begin service under one of the Duke's captains. A man-at-arms in the splendid suite of the Burgundian Dukes was generally of good birth, and was attended by two grooms and a page when in the field; his pay was fairly sufficient, and his accoutrements and arms were required to be such as to do honour to his employer. It was the refuge sooner or later of many a Lancastrian, and Leonard, who doubted of the regularity of his uncle's supplies, decided that he could do no better for himself while waiting for better times for his Queen, though Master Lambert told him that he need not distress himself, there were ample means for him still.

Grisell spun and sewed for his outfit, with a strange sad pleasure in working for him, and she was absolutely proud of him when he stood before her, perfectly recovered, with the glow of health on his cheek and a light in his eye, his length of limb arrayed in his own armour, furbished and mended, his bright helmet alone new and of her own providing (out of her mother's pearl necklace), his surcoat and silken scarf all her own embroidering. As he truly said, he made a much finer appearance than he had done on the morn of his melancholy knighthood, in the poverty-stricken army of King Henry at Northampton.

"Thanks," he said, with a courteous bow, "to his good friends and hosts, who had a wonderful power over the purse." He added special thanks to "Mistress Grisell for her deft stitchery," and she responded with down-cast face, and a low courtesy, while her heart throbbed high.

Such a cavalier was sure of enlistment, and Leonard came to take leave of his host, and announced that he had been sent off with his friend to garrison Neufchatel, where the castle, being a border one, was always carefully watched over.

His friends at Bruges rejoiced in his absence, since it prevented his knowledge of the arrival of his beloved

Queen Margaret and her son at Sluys, with only seven attendants, denuded of almost everything, having lost her last castles, and sometimes having had to exist on a single herring a day.

Perhaps Leonard would have laid his single sword at her feet if he had known of her presence, but tidings travelled slowly, and before they ever reached Neufchatel the Duke had bestowed on her wherewithal to continue her journey to her father's Court at Bar.

However, he did not move. Indeed be did not hear of the Queen's journey to Scotland and fresh attempt till all had been again lost at Hedgeley Moor and Hexham. He was so good and efficient a man-at-arms that he rose in promotion, and attracted the notice of the Count of Charolais, the eldest son of the Duke, who made him one of his own bodyguard. His time was chiefly spent in escorting the Count from one castle or city to another, but whenever Charles the Bold was at Bruges, Leonard came to the sign of the Green Serpent not only for lodging, nor only to take up the money that Lambert had in charge for him, but as to a home where he was sure of a welcome, and of kindly woman's care of his wardrobe, and where he grew more and more to look to the sympathy and understanding of his English and Burgundian interests alike, which he found in the maiden who sat by the hearth.

From time to time old Ridley came to see her. He was clad in a pilgrim's gown and broad hat, and looked much older. He had had free quarters at Willimoteswick, but the wild young Borderers had not suited his old age well, except one clerkly youth, who reminded him of little Bernard, and who, later, was the patron of his nephew, the famous Nicolas. He had thus set out on pilgrimage, as the best means of visiting his dear lady. The first time he came, under his robe he carried a girdle, where was sewn up a small supply from Father Copeland for his nephew, and another sum, very meagre, but collected from the faithful retainers of Whitburn for their lady. He meant to visit the Three Kings at Cologne, and then to go on to St. Gall, and to the various nearer shrines in France, but to return again to see Grisell; and from time to time he showed his honest face, more and more weather-beaten, though a pilgrim was never in want; but Grisell delighted in preparing new gowns, clean linen, and fresh hats for him.

Public events passed while she still lived and worked in the Apothecary's house at Bruges. There were wars in which Sir Leonard Copeland had his share, not very perilous to a knight in full armour, but falling very heavily on poor citizens. Bruges, however, was at peace and exceedingly prosperous, with its fifty-two guilds of citizens, and wonderful trade and wealth. The bells seemed to be always chiming from its many beautiful steeples, and there was one convent lately founded which began to have a special interest for Grisell.

It was the house of the Hospitalier Grey Sisters, which if not actually founded had been much embellished by Isabel of Portugal, the wife of the Duke of Burgundy. Philip, though called the Good, from his genial manners, and bounteous liberality, was a man of violent temper and terrible severity when offended. He had a fierce quarrel with his only son, who was equally hot tempered. The Duchess took part with her son, and fell under such furious displeasure from her husband that she retired into the house of Grey Sisters. She was first cousin once removed to Henry VI. - her mother, the admirable Philippa, having been a daughter of John of Gaunt - and she was the sister of the noble Princes, King Edward of Portugal, Henry the great voyager, and Ferdinand the Constant Prince; and she had never been thoroughly at home or happy in Flanders, where her husband was of a far coarser nature than her own family; and, in her own words, after many years, she always felt herself a stranger.

Some of Grisell's lace had found its way to the convent, and was at once recognised by her as English, such as her mother had always prized. She wished to give the Chaplain a set of robes adorned with lace after a pattern of her own devising, bringing in the five crosses of Portugal, with appropriate wreaths of flowers and emblems. Being told that the English maiden in Master Groot's house could devise her own patterns, she desired to see her and explain the design in person.

CHAPTER XXV

THE OLD DUCHESS

Temples that rear their stately heads on high,
Canals that intersect the fertile plain,
Wide streets and squares, with many a court and hall,
Spacious and undefined, but ancient all.

SOUTHEY, Pilgrimage to Waterloo.

The kind couple of Groots were exceedingly solicitous about Grisell's appearance before the Duchess, and much concerned that she could not be induced to wear the head-gear a foot or more in height, with veils depending from the peak, which was the fashion of the Netherlands. Her black robe and hood, permitted but not enjoined in the external or third Order of St. Francis, were, as usual, her dress, and under it might be seen a face, with something peculiar on one side, but still full of sweetness and intelligence; and the years of comfort and quiet had, in spite of anxiety, done much to obliterate the likeness to a cankered oak gall. Lambert wanted to drench her with perfumes, but she only submitted to have a little essence in the pouncet box given her long ago by Lady Margaret at their parting at Amesbury. Master Groot himself chose to conduct her on this first great occasion, and they made their way to the old gateway, sculptured above with figures that still remain, into the great cloistered court, with its chapel, chapter-house, and splendid great airy hall, in which the Hospital Sisters received their patients.

They were seen flitting about, giving a general effect of gray, whence they were known as Soeurs Grises, though, in fact, their dress was white, with a black hood and mantle. The Duchess, however, lived in a set of chambers on one side of the court, which she had built and fitted for herself.

A lay sister became Grisell's guide, and just then, coming down from the Duchess's apartments, with a board with a chalk sketch in his hand, appeared a young man, whom Groot greeted as Master Hans Memling, and who had been receiving orders, and showing designs to the Duchess for the ornamentation of the convent, which in later years he so splendidly carried out. With him Lambert remained.

There was a broad stone stair, leading to a large apartment hung with stamped Spanish leather, representing the history of King David, and with a window, glazed as usual below with circles and lozenges, but the upper part glowing with coloured glass. At the farther end was a dais with a sort of throne, like the tester and canopy of a four-post bed, with curtains looped up at each side. Here the Duchess sat, surrounded by her ladies, all in the sober dress suitable with monastic life.

Grisell knew her duty too well not to kneel down when admitted. A dark-complexioned lady came to lead her forward, and directed her to kneel twice on her way to the Duchess. She obeyed, and in that indescribable

manner which betrayed something of her breeding, so
that after her second obeisance, the manner of the lady
altered visibly from what it had been at first as to a
burgher maiden. The wealth and luxury of the citizen
world of the Low Countries caused the proud and
jealous nobility to treat them with the greater distance
of manner. And, as Grisell afterwards learnt, this was
Isabel de Souza, Countess of Poitiers, a Portuguese
lady who had come over with her Infanta; and whose
daughter produced Les Honneurs de la Cour, the most
wonderful of all descriptions of the formalities of the
Court.

Grisell remained kneeling on the steps of the dais,
while the Duchess addressed her in much more
imperfect Flemish than she could by this time speak
herself.

"You are the lace weaver, maiden. Can you speak
French?"

"Oui, si madame, son Altese le veut," replied Grisell,
for her tongue had likewise become accustomed to
French in this city of many tongues.

"This is English make," said the Duchess, not with a
very good French accent either, looking at the
specimens handed by her lady. "Are you English?"

"So please your Highness, I am."

"An exile?" the Princess added kindly.

"Yes, madame. All my family perished in our wars,
and I owe shelter to the good Apothecary, Master
Lambert."

"Purveyor of drugs to the sisters. Yes, I have heard of him;" and she then proceeded with her orders, desiring to see the first piece Grisell should produce in the pattern she wished, which was to be of roses in honour of St. Elizabeth of Hungary, whom the Peninsular Isabels reckoned as their namesake and patroness.

It was a pattern which would require fresh pricking out, and much skill; but Grisell thought she could accomplish it, and took her leave, kissing the Duchess's hand - a great favour to be granted to her - curtseying three times, and walking backwards, after the old training that seemed to come back to her with the atmosphere.

Master Lambert was overjoyed when he heard all. "Now you will find your way back to your proper station and rank," he said.

"It may do more than that," said Grisell. "If I could plead his cause."

Lambert only sighed. "I would fain your way was not won by a base, mechanical art," he said.

"Out on you, my master. The needle and the bobbin are unworthy of none; and as to the honour of the matter, what did Sir Leonard tell us but that the Countess of Oxford, as now she is, was maintaining her husband by her needle?" and Grisell ended with a sigh at thought of the happy woman whose husband knew of, and was grateful for, her toils.

The pattern needed much care, and Lambert induced Hans Memling himself, who drew it so that it could be pricked out for the cushion. In after times it might have been held a greater honour to work from his pattern than for the Duchess, who sent to inquire after it more than once, and finally desired that Mistress Grisell should bring her cushion and show her progress.

She was received with all the same ceremonies as before, and even the small fragment that was finished delighted the Princess, who begged to see her at work. As it could not well be done kneeling, a footstool, covered in tapestry with the many Burgundian quarterings, was brought, and here Grisell was seated, the Duchess bending over her, and asking questions as her fingers flew, at first about the work, but afterwards, "Where did you learn this art, maiden?"

"At Wilton, so please your Highness. The nunnery of St. Edith, near to Salisbury."

"St. Edith! I think my mother, whom the Saints rest, spoke of her; but I have not heard of her in Portugal nor here. Where did she suffer?"

"She was not martyred, madame, but she has a fair legend."

And on encouragement Grisell related the legend of St. Edith and the christening.

"You speak well, maiden," said the Duchess. "It is easy to perceive that you are convent trained. Have the wars in England hindered your being professed?"

"Nay, madame; it was the Proctor of the Italian Abbess."

Therewith the inquiries of the Duchess elicited all

Charlotte M. Yonge

Grisell's early story, with the exception of her name and whose was the iron that caused the explosion, and likewise of her marriage, and the accusation of sorcery. That male heirs of the opposite party should have expelled the orphan heiress was only too natural an occurrence. Nor did Grisell conceal her home; but Whitburn was an impossible word to Portuguese lips, and Dacre they pronounced after its crusading derivation De Acor.

CHAPTER XXVI

THE DUKE'S DEATH

Wither one Rose, and let the other flourish;
If you contend, a thousand lives must wither.

SHAKESPEARE, King Henry VI., Part III.

So time went on, and the rule of the House of York in
England seemed established, while the exiles had
settled down in Burgundy, Grisell to her lace pillow,
Leonard to the suite of the Count de Charolais. Indeed
there was reason to think that he had come to
acquiesce in the change of dynasty, or at any rate to
think it unwise and cruel to bring on another desperate
civil war. In fact, many of the Red Rose party were
making their peace with Edward IV. Meanwhile the
Duchess Isabel became extremely fond of Grisell, and
often summoned her to come and work by her side,
and talk to her; and thus came on the summer of 1467,
when Duke Philip returned from the sack of unhappy
Dinant in a weakened state, and soon after was taken
fatally ill. All the city of Bruges watched in anxiety for
tidings, for the kindly Duke was really loved where his
hand did not press. One evening during the suspense
when Master Lambert was gone out to gather tidings,
there was the step with clank of spurs which had
grown familiar, and Leonard Copeland strode in hot

and dusty, greeting Vrow Clemence as usual with a touch of the hand and inclination of the head, and Grisell with hand and courteous voice, as he threw himself on the settle, heated and weary, and began with tired fingers to unfasten his heavy steel cap.

Grisell hastened to help him, Clemence to fetch a cup of cooling Rhine wine. "There, thanks, mistress. We have ridden all day from Ghent, in the heat and dust, and after all the Count got before us."

"To the Duke?"

"Ay! He was like one demented at tidings of his father's sickness. Say what they will of hot words and fierce passages between them, that father and son have hearts loving one another truly."

"It is well they should agree at the last," said Grisell, "or the Count will carry with him the sorest of memories."

And indeed Charles the Bold was on his knees beside the bed of his speechless father in an agony of grief.

Presently all the bells in Bruges began to clash out their warning that a soul was passing to the unseen land, and Grisell made signs to Clemence, while Leonard lifted himself upright, and all breathed the same for the mighty Prince as for the poorest beggar, the intercession for the dying. Then the solemn note became a knell, and their prayer changed to the De Profundis, "Out of the depths."

Presently Lambert Groot came in, grave and saddened, with the intelligence that Philip the Good had departed in peace, with his wife and son on either side of him, and his little granddaughter kneeling beside the Duchess.

There was bitter weeping all over Bruges, and soon all over Flanders and the other domains united under the Dukedom of Burgundy, for though Philip had often deeply erred, he had been a fair ruler, balancing discordant interests justly, and maintaining peace, while all that was splendid or luxurious prospered and throve under him. There was a certain dread of the future under his successor.

"A better man at heart," said Leonard, who had learnt to love the Count de Charolais. "He loathes the vices and revelry that have stained the Court."

"That is true," said Lambert. "Yet he is a man of violence, and with none of the skill and dexterity with which Duke Philip steered his course."

"A plague on such skill," muttered Leonard. "Caring solely for his own gain, not for the right!"

"Yet your Count has a heavy hand," said Lambert. "Witness Dinant! unhappy Dinant."

"The rogues insulted his mother," said Leonard. "He offered them terms which they would not have in their stubborn pride! But speak not of that! I never saw the like in England. There we strike at the great, not at the small. Ah well, with all our wars and troubles England was the better place to live in. Shall we ever see it more?"

There was something delightful to Grisell in that "we,"

Charlotte M. Yonge

but she made answer, "So far as I hear, there has been quiet there for the last two years under King Edward."

"Ay, and after all he has the right of blood," said Leonard. "Our King Henry is a saint, and Queen Margaret a peerless dame of romance, but since I have come to years of understanding I have seen that they neither had true claim of inheritance nor power to rule a realm."

"Then would you make your peace with the White Rose?"

"The rose en soleil that wrought us so much evil at Mortimer's Cross? Methinks I would. I never swore allegiance to King Henry. My father was still living when last I saw that sweet and gracious countenance which I must defend for love and reverence' sake."

"And he knighted you," said Grisell.

"True," with a sharp glance, as if he wondered how she was aware of the fact; "but only as my father's heir. My poor old house and tenants! I would I knew how they fare; but mine uncle sends me no letters, though he does supply me."

"Then you do not feel bound in honour to Lancaster?" said Grisell.

"Nay; I did not stir or strive to join the Queen when last she called up the Scots - the Scots indeed! - to aid her. I could not join them in a foray on England. I fear me she will move heaven and earth again when her son is of age to bear arms; but my spirit rises against allies among Scots or French, and I cannot think it well to bring back bloodshed and slaughter."

"I shall pray for peace," said Grisell. All this was happiness to her, as she felt that he was treating her with confidence. Would she ever be nearer to him?

He was a graver, more thoughtful man at seven and twenty than he had been at the time of his hurried marriage, and had conversed with men of real understanding of the welfare of their country. Such talks as these made Grisell feel that she could look up to him as most truly her lord and guide. But how was it with the fair Eleanor, and whither did his heart incline? An English merchant, who came for spices, had said that the Lord Audley had changed sides, and it was thus probable that the damsel was bestowed in marriage to a Yorkist; but there was no knowing, nor did Grisell dare to feel her way to discovering whether Leonard knew, or felt himself still bound to constancy, outwardly and in heart.

Every one was taken up with the funeral solemnities of Duke Philip; he was to be finally interred with his father and grandfather in the grand tombs at Dijon, but for the present the body was to be placed in the Church of St. Donatus at Bruges, at night.

Sir Leonard rode at a foot's pace in the troop of men-at-arms, all in full armour, which glanced in the light of the sixteen hundred torches which were borne before, behind, and in the midst of the procession, which escorted the bier. Outside the coffin, arrayed in ducal coronet and robes, with the Golden Fleece collar round the neck, lay the exact likeness of the aged Duke, and on shields around the pall, as well as on banners borne waving aloft, were the armorial bearings

Charlotte M. Yonge

of all his honours, his four dukedoms, seven counties, lordships innumerable, besides the banners of all the guilds carried to do him honour.

More than twenty prelates were present, and shared in the mass, which began in the morning hour, and in the requiem. The heralds of all the domains broke their white staves and threw them on the bier, proclaiming that Philip, lord of all these lands, was deceased. Then, as in the case of royalty, Charles his son was proclaimed; and the organ led an acclamation of jubilee from all the assembly which filled the church, and a shout as of thunder arose, "Vivat Carolus."

Charles knelt meanwhile with hands clasped over his brow, silent, immovable. Was he crushed at thought of the whirlwinds of passion that had raged between him and the father whom he had loved all the time? or was there on him the weight of a foreboding that he, though free from the grosser faults of his father, would never win and keep hearts in the same manner, and that a sad, tumultuous, troubled career and piteous, untimely end lay before him?

His mother, Grisell's Duchess, according to the rule of the Court, lay in bed for six weeks - at least she was bound to lie there whenever she was not in entire privacy. The room and bed were hung with black, but a white covering was over her, and she was fully dressed in the black and white weeds of royal widowhood. The light of day was excluded, and hosts of wax candles burnt around.

Grisell did not see her during this first period of stately mourning, but she heard that the good lady had spent her time in weeping and praying for her husband, all the more earnestly that she had little cause personally to mourn him.

Charlotte M. Yonge

CHAPTER XXVII

FORGET ME NOT

And added, of her wit,
A border fantasy of branch and flower,
And yellow-throated nestling in the nest.

TENNYSON, Elaine.

The Duchess Isabel sent for Grisell as soon as the rules
of etiquette permitted, and her own mind was free, to
attend to the suite of lace hangings, with which much
progress had been made in the interval. She was in the
palace now, greatly honoured, for her son loved her
with devoted affection, and Grisell had to pass through
tapestry-hung halls and chambers, one after another,
with persons in mourning, all filled with men-at-arms
first, then servants still in black dresses. Next pages
and squires, knights of the lady, and lastly ladies in
black velvet, who sat at their work, with a chaplain
reading to them. One of these, the Countess of Poitiers,
whom Grisell had known at the Grey Sisters' convent,
rose, graciously received her obeisance, and conducted
her into the great State bedroom, likewise very sombre,
with black hangings worked and edged, however, with
white, and the window was permitted to let in the light
of day. The bed was raised on steps in an alcove, and
was splendidly draped and covered with black

embroidered with white, but the Duchess did not occupy it. A curtain was lifted, and she came forward in her deepest robes of widowhood, leading her little granddaughter Mary, a child of eight or nine years old. Grisell knelt to kiss the hands of each, and the Duchess said -

"Good Griselda, it is long since I have seen you. Have you finished the border?"

"Yes, your Highness; and I have begun the edging of the corporal."

The Duchess looked at the work with admiration, and bade the little Mary, the damsel of Burgundy, look on and see how the dainty web was woven, while she signed the maker to seat herself on a step of the alcove.

When the child's questions and interest were exhausted, and she began to be somewhat perilously curious about the carved weights of the bobbins, her grandmother sent her to play with the ladies in the ante-room, desiring Grisell to continue the work. After a few kindly words the Duchess said, "The poor child is to have a stepdame so soon as the year of mourning is passed. May she be good to her! Hath the rumour thereof reached you in the city, Maid Griselda, that my son is in treaty with your English King, though he loves not the house of York? But princely alliances must be looked for in marriage."

"Madge!" exclaimed Grisell; then colouring, "I should say the Lady Margaret of York."

"You knew her?"

"Oh! I knew her. We loved each other well in the Lord of Salisbury's house! There never was a maid whom I knew or loved like her!"

"In the Count of Salisbury's house," repeated the Duchess. "Were you there as the Lady Margaret's fellow-pupil?" she said, as though perceiving that her lace maker must be of higher quality than she had supposed.

"It was while my father was alive, madame, and before her father had fixed his eyes on the throne, your Highness."

"And your father was, you said, the knight De - De - D'Acor."

"So please you, madame," said Grisell kneeling, "not to mention my poor name to the lady."

"We are a good way from speech of her," said the Duchess smiling. "Our year of doole must pass, and mayhap the treaty will not hold in the meantime. The King of France would fain hinder it. But if the Demoiselle loved you of old would she not give you preferment in her train if she knew?"

"Oh! madame, I pray you name me not till she be here! There is much that hangs on it, more than I can tell at present, without doing harm; but I have a petition to prefer to her."

"An affair of true love," said the Duchess smiling.

"I know not. Oh! ask me not, madame!"

When Grisell was dismissed, she began designing a pattern, in which in spray after spray of rich point, she displayed in the pure frostwork-like web, the Daisy of Margaret, the Rose of York, and moreover, combined therewith, the saltire of Nevil and the three scallops of Dacre, and each connected with ramifications of the forget-me-not flower shaped like the turquoises of her pouncet box, and with the letter G to be traced by ingenious eyes, though the uninitiated might observe nothing.

She had plenty of time, though the treaty soon made it as much of a certainty as royal betrothals ever were, but it was not till July came round again that Bruges was in a crisis of the fever of preparation to receive the bride. Sculptors, painters, carvers were desperately at work at the Duke's palace. Weavers, tapestry-workers, embroiderers, sempstresses were toiling day and night, armourers and jewellers had no rest, and the bright July sunshine lay glittering on the canals, graceful skiffs, and gorgeous barges, and bringing out in full detail the glories of the architecture above, the tapestry-hung windows in the midst, the gaily-clad Vrows beneath, while the bells rang out their merriest carillons from every steeple, whence fluttered the banners of the guilds.

The bride, escorted by Sir Antony Wydville, was to land at Sluys, and Duchess Isabel, with little Mary, went to receive her.

"Will you go with me as one of my maids, or as a tirewoman perchance?" asked the Duchess kindly.

Grisell fell on her knee and thanked her, but begged to be permitted to remain where she was until the bride should have some leisure. And indeed her doubts and suspense grew more overwhelming. As she freshly trimmed and broidered Leonard's surcoat and sword-belt, she heard one of the many gossips who delighted to recount the members of the English suite as picked up from the subordinates of the heralds and pursuivants who had to marshal the procession and order the banquet. "Fair ladies too," he said, "from England. There is the Lord Audley's daughter with her father. They say she is the very pearl of beauties. We shall see whether our fair dames do not surpass her."

"The Lord Audley's daughter did you say?" asked Grisell.

"His daughter, yea; but she is a widow, bearing in her lozenge, per pale with Audley, gules three herrings haurient argent, for Heringham. She is one of the Duchess Margaret's dames-of-honour."

To Grisell it sounded like her doom on one side, the crisis of her self-sacrifice, and the opening of Leonard's happiness on the other.

CHAPTER XXVIII

THE PAGEANT

When I may read of tilts in days of old,
And tourneys graced by chieftains of renown,
Fair dames, grave citoyens, and warriors bold -
If fancy would pourtray some stately town,
Which for such pomp fit theatre would be,
Fair Bruges, I shall then remember thee.

SOUTHEY, Pilgrimage to Waterloo.

Leonard Copeland was in close attendance on the Duke, and could not give a moment to visit his friends at the Green Serpent, so that there was no knowing how the presence of the Lady of Heringham affected him. Duke Charles rode out to meet his bride at the little town of Damme, and here the more important portions of the betrothal ceremony took place, after which he rode back alone to the Cour des Princes, leaving to the bride all the splendour of the entrance.

The monastic orders were to be represented in the procession. The Grey Sisters thought they had an especial claim, and devised the presenting a crown of white roses at the gates, and with great pleasure Grisell contributed the best of Master Lambert's lovely white Provence roses to complete the garland, which was

　　　　Charlotte M. Yonge

carried by the youngest novice, a fair white rosebud herself.

Every one all along the line of the tall old houses was hanging from window to window rich tapestries of many dyes, often with gold and silver thread. The trades and guilds had renewed their signs, banners and pennons hung from every abode entitled to their use, garlands of bright flowers stretched here and there and everywhere. All had been in a frenzy of preparation for many days past, and the final touches began with the first hours of light in the long, summer morning. To Grisell's great delight, Cuthbert Ridley plodded in at the hospitable door of the Green Serpent the night before. "Ah! my ladybird," said he, "in good health as ever."

"All the better for seeing you, mine old friend," she cried. "I thought you were far away at Compostella."

"So verily I was. Here's St. James's cockle to wit - Santiago as they call him there, and show the stone coffin he steered across the sea. No small miracle that! And I've crossed France, and looked at many a field of battle of the good old times, and thought and said a prayer for the brave knights who broke lances there. But as I was making for St. Martha's cave in Provence, I met a friar, who told me of the goodly gathering there was like to be here; and I would fain see whether I could hap upon old friends, or at any rate hear a smack of our kindly English tongue, so I made the best of my way hither."

"In good time," said Lambert. "You will take the lady and the housewife to the stoop at Master Caxton's house, where he has promised them seats whence they may view the entrance. I myself am bound to walk with my fellows of the Apothecaries' Society, and it will be well for them to have another guard in the throng, besides old Anton."

"Nay, but my garb scarce befits the raree show," said Ridley, looking at his russet gown.

"We will see to that anon," said Lambert; and ere supper was over, old Anton had purveyed a loose blue gown from the neighbouring merchants, with gold lace seams and girdle, peaked boots, and the hideous brimless hat which was then highly fashionable. Ridley's trusty sword he had always worn under his pilgrim's gown, and with the dagger always used as a knife, he made his appearance once more as a squire of degree, still putting the scallop into his hat, in honour of Dacre as well as of St. James.

The party had to set forth very early in the morning, slowly gliding along several streets in a barge, watching the motley crowds thronging banks and bridges - a far more brilliant crowd than in these later centuries, since both sexes were alike gay in plumage. From every house, even those out of the line of the procession, hung tapestry, or coloured cloths, and the garlands of flowers, of all bright lines, with their fresh greenery, were still unfaded by the clear morning sun, while joyous carillons echoed and re-echoed from the belfry and all the steeples. Ridley owned that he had never seen the like since King Harry rode home from Agincourt - perhaps hardly even then, for Bruges was at the height of its splendour, as were the Burgundian Dukes at the very climax of their magnificence.

After landing from the barge Ridley, with Grisell on

his arm, and Anton with his mistress, had a severe struggle with the crowd before they gained the ascent of the stoop, where the upper steps had been railed in, and seats arranged under the shelter of the projecting roof.

Master Caxton was a gray-eyed, thin-cheeked, neatly-made Kentishman, who had lived long abroad, and was always ready to make an Englishman welcome. He listened politely to Grisell's introduction of Master Ridley, exchanged silent greetings with Vrow Clemence, and insisted on their coming into the chamber within, where a repast of cold pasty, march-pane, strawberries, and wine, awaited them - to be eaten while as yet there was nothing to see save the expectant multitudes.

Moreover, he wanted to show Mistress Grisell, as one of the few who cared for it, the manuscripts he had collected on the history of Troy town, and likewise the strange machine on which he was experimenting for multiplying copies of the translation he had in hand, with blocks for the woodcuts which Grisell could not in conscience say would be as beautiful as the gorgeous illuminations of his books.

Acclamations summoned them to the front, of course at first to see only scattered bodies of the persons on the way to meet the bride at the gate of St. Croix.

By and by, however, came the "gang," as Ridley called it, in earnest. Every body of ecclesiastics was there: monks and friars, black, white, and gray; nuns, black, white, and blue; the clergy in their richest robes, with costly crucifixes of gold, silver, and ivory held aloft, and reliquaries of the most exquisite workmanship, sparkling with precious jewels, diamond, ruby, emerald, and sapphire flashing in the sun; the fifty-two guilds in gowns, each headed by their Master and their banner, gorgeous in tint, but with homely devices, such as stockings, saw and compasses, weavers' shuttles, and the like. Master Lambert looked up and nodded a smile from beneath a banner with Apollo and the Python, which Ridley might be excused for taking for St. Michael and the Dragon. The Mayor in scarlet, white fur and with gold collar, surrounded by his burgomasters in almost equally radiant garments, marched on.

Next followed the ducal household, trumpets and all sorts of instruments before them, making the most festive din, through which came bursts of the joy bells. Violet and black arrayed the inferiors, setting off the crimson satin pourpoints of the higher officers, on whose brimless hats each waved with a single ostrich plume in a shining brooch.

Then came more instruments, and a body of gay green archers; next heralds and pursuivants, one for each of the Duke's domains, glittering back and front in the tabard of his county's armorial bearings, and with its banner borne beside him. Then a division of the Duke's bodyguard, all like himself in burnished armour with scarves across them. The nobles of Burgundy, Flanders, Hainault, Holland, and Alsace, the most splendid body then existing, came in endless numbers, their horses, feather-crested as well as themselves, with every bridle tinkling with silver bells, and the animals invisible all but their heads and tails under their magnificent housings, while the knights seemed to be pillars of radiance. Yet even more gorgeous were the knights of the Golden Fleece, who left between them a lane in which moved six white horses, caparisoned in cloth of gold, drawing an open litter in which sat, as on a throne, herself dazzling in cloth of silver, the brown-eyed Margaret of old, her dark hair bride fashion flowing on her shoulders, and around it a marvello-usly-glancing diamond coronet, above it, however, the wreath of white roses, which her own hands had placed there when presented by the novice. Clemence squeezed Grisell's hand with delight as she recognised her own white rose, the finest of the garland.

Immediately after the car came Margaret's English attendants, the stately, handsome Antony Wydville riding nearest to her, and then a bevy of dames and damsels on horseback, but moving so slowly that Grisell had full time to discover the silver herrings on the caparisons of one of the palfreys, and then to raise her eyes to the face of the tall stately lady whose long veil, flowing down from her towered head-gear, by no means concealed a beautiful complexion and fair perfect features, such as her own could never have rivalled even if they had never been defaced. Her heart sank within her, everything swam before her eyes, she scarcely saw the white doves let loose from the triumphant arch beyond to greet the royal lady, and was first roused by Ridley's exclamation as the knights with their attendants began to pass.

"Ha! the lad kens me! 'Tis Harry Featherstone as I live."

Much more altered in these seven years than was Cuthbert Ridley, there rode as a fully-equipped squire in the rear of a splendid knight, Harry Featherstone, the survivor of the dismal Bridge of Wakefield. He was lowering his lance in greeting, but there was no knowing whether it was to Ridley or to Grisell, or whether he recognised her, as she wore her veil far over her face.

This to Grisell closed the whole. She did not see the figure which was more to her than all the rest, for he was among the knights and guards waiting at the Cour des Princes to receive the bride when the final ceremonies of the marriage were to be performed.

Ridley declared his intention of seeking out young Featherstone, but Grisell impressed on him that she wished to remain unknown for the present, above all to Sir Leonard Copeland, and he had been quite sufficiently alarmed by the accusations of sorcery to believe in the danger of her becoming known among the English.

"More by token," said he, "that the house of this Master Caxton as you call him seems to me no canny haunt. Tell me what you will of making manifold good books or bad, I'll never believe but that Dr. Faustus and the Devil hatched the notion between them for the bewilderment of men's brains and the slackening of their hands."

Thus Ridley made little more attempt to persuade his young lady to come forth to the spectacles of the next fortnight to which he rushed, through crowds and jostling, to behold, with the ardour of an old warrior, the various tilts and tourneys, though he grumbled that they were nothing but child's play and vain show, no earnest in them fit for a man.

Clemence, however, was all eyes, and revelled in the sight of the wonders, the view of the Tree of Gold, and the champion thereof in the lists of the Hotel de Ville, and again, some days later, of the banquet, when the table decorations were mosaic gardens with silver trees, laden with enamelled fruit, and where, as an interlude, a whale sixty feet long made its entrance and emitted from its jaws a troop of Moorish youths and maidens, who danced a saraband to the sound of tambourines and cymbals! Such scenes were bliss to the deaf housewife, and would enliven the silent world of her memory all the rest of her life.

The Duchess Isabel had retired to the Grey Sisters, such scenes being inappropriate to her mourning, and besides her apartments being needed for the influx of guests. There, in early morning, before the revels began, Grisell ventured to ask for an audience, and was permitted to follow the Duchess when she returned from mass to her own apartments.

"Ah! my lace weaver. Have you had your share in the revels and pageantries?"

"I saw the procession, so please your Grace."

"And your old playmate in her glory?"

"Yea, madame. It almost forestalled the glories of Heaven!"

"Ah! child, may the aping of such glory beforehand not unfit us for the veritable everlasting glories, when all these things shall be no more."

The Duchess clasped her hands, almost as a foreboding of the day when her son's corpse should lie, forsaken, gashed, and stripped, beside the marsh.

But she turned to Grisell asking if she had come with any petition.

"Only, madame, that it would please your Highness to put into the hands of the new Duchess herself, this offering, without naming me."

She produced her exquisite fabric, which was tied with ribbons of blue and silver in an outer case, worked with the White Rose.

The Dowager-Duchess exclaimed, "Nay, but this is more beauteous than all you have wrought before. Ah! here is your own device! I see there is purpose in these patterns of your web. And am I not to name you?"

"I pray your Highness to be silent, unless the Duchess should divine the worker. Nay, it is scarce to be thought that she will."

"Yet you have put the flower that my English mother called 'Forget-me-not.' Ah, maiden, has it a purpose?"

"Madame, madame, ask me no questions. Only remember in your prayers to ask that I may do the right," said Grisell, with clasped hands and weeping eyes.

CHAPTER XXIX

DUCHESS MARGARET

I beheld the pageants splendid, that adorned those
days of old; Stately dames, like queens attended,
knights who bore the Fleece of Gold.

LONGFELLOW, The Belfry of Bruges.

In another week the festivities were over, and she waited anxiously, dreading each day more and more that her gift had been forgotten or misunderstood, or that her old companion disdained or refused to take notice of her; then trying to console herself by remembering the manifold engagements and distractions of the bride.

Happily, Grisell thought, Ridley was absent when Leonard Copeland came one evening to supper. He was lodged among the guards of the Duke in the palace, and had much less time at his disposal than formerly, for Duke Charles insisted on the most strict order and discipline among all his attendants. Moreover, there were tokens of enmity on the part of the French on the border of the Somme, and Leonard expected to be despatched to the camp which was being formed there. He was out of spirits. The sight and speech of so many of his countrymen had increased the longing for home.

"I loathe the mincing French and the fat Flemish tongues," he owned, when Master Lambert was out of hearing. "I should feel at home if I could but hear an honest carter shout 'Woa' to his horses."

"Did you have any speech with the ladies?" asked Grisell.

"I? No! What reck they of a poor knight adventurer?"

"Methought all the chivalry were peers, and that a belted knight was a comrade for a king," said Grisell.

"Ay, in the days of the Round Table; but when Dukes and Counts, and great Marquesses and Barons swarm like mayflies by a trout stream, what chance is there that a poor, landless exile will have a word or a glance?"

Did this mean that the fair Eleanor had scorned him? Grisell longed to know, but for that very reason she faltered when about to ask, and turned her query into one whether he had heard any news of his English relations.

"My good uncle at Wearmouth hath been dead these four years - so far as I can gather. Amply must he have supplied Master Groot. I must account with him. For mine inheritance I can gather nothing clearly. I fancy the truth is that George Copeland, who holds it, is little better than a reiver on either side, and that King Edward might grant it back to me if I paid my homage, save that he is sworn never to pardon any who had a share in the death of his brother of Rutland."

"You had not! I know you had not!"

"Hurt Ned? I'd as soon have hurt my own brother! Nay, I got this blow from Clifford for coming between," said he, pushing back his hair so as to show a mark near his temple. "But how did you know?"

"Harry Featherstone told me." She had all but said, "My father's squire."

"You knew Featherstone? Belike when he was at Whitburn. He is here now; a good man of his hands," muttered Leonard. "Anyway the King believes I had a hand in that cruel business of Wakefield Bridge, and nought but his witness would save my neck if once I ventured into England - if that would. So I may resign myself to be the Duke's captain of archers for the rest of my days. Heigh ho! And a lonely man; I fear me in debt to good Master Lambert, or may be to Mistress Grisell, to whom I owe more than coin will pay. Ha! was that - " interrupting himself, for a trumpet blast was ringing out at intervals, the signal of summons to the men-at-arms. Leonard started up, waved farewell, and rushed off.

The summons proved to be a call to the men-at-arms to attend the Duke early the next morning on an expedition to visit his fortresses in Picardy, and as the household of the Green Serpent returned from mass, they heard the tramp and clatter, and saw the armour flash in the sun as the troop passed along the main street, and became visible at the opening of that up which they walked.

The next day came a summons from the convent of the Grey Sisters that Mistress Griselda was to attend the

Duchess Isabel.

She longed to fly through the air, but her limbs trembled. Indeed, she shook so that she could not stand still nor walk slowly. She hurried on so that the lay sister who had been sent for her was quite out of breath, and panted after her within gasps of "Stay! stay, mistress! No bear is after us! She runs as though a mad ox had got loose!"

Her heart was wild enough for anything! She might have to hear from her kind Duchess that all was vain and unnoticed.

Up the stair she went, to the accustomed chamber, where an additional chair was on the dais under the canopy, the half circle of ladies as usual, but before she had seen more with her dazzled, swimming eyes, even as she rose from her first genuflection, she found herself in a pair of soft arms, kisses rained on her cheeks and brow, and there was a tender cry in her own tongue of "My Grisell! my dear old Grisell! I have found you at last! Oh! that was good in you. I knew the forget-me-nots, and all your little devices. Ah!" as Grisell, unable to speak for tears of joy, held up the pouncet box, the childish gift.

The soft pink velvet bodice girdled and clasped with diamonds was pressed to her, the deep hanging silken sleeves were round her, the white satin broidered skirt swept about her feet, the pearl-edged matronly cap on the youthful head leant fondly against her, as Margaret led her up, still in her embrace, and cried, "It is she, it is she! Dear belle mere, thanks indeed for bringing us together!"

The Countess of Poitiers looked on scandalised at English impulsiveness, and the elder Duchess herself looked for a moment stiff, as her lace-maker slipped to her knees to kiss her hand and murmur her thanks.

"Let me look at you," cried Margaret. "Ah! have you recovered that terrible mishap? By my troth, 'tis nearly gone. I should never have found it out had I not known!"

This was rather an exaggeration, but joy did make a good deal of difference in Grisell's face, and the Duchess Margaret was one of the most eager and warm-hearted people living, fervent alike in love and in hate, ready both to act on slight evidence for those whose cause she took up, and to nourish bitter hatred against the enemies of her house.

"Now, tell me all," she continued in English. "I heard that you had been driven out of Wilton, and my uncle of Warwick had sped you northward. How is it that you are here, weaving lace like any mechanical sempstress? Nay, nay! I cannot listen to you on your knees. We have hugged one another too often for that."

Grisell, with the elder Duchess's permission, seated herself on the cushion at Margaret's feet. "Speak English," continued the bride. "I am wearying already of French! Ma belle mere, you will not find fault. You know a little of our own honest tongue."

Duchess Isabel smiled, and Grisell, in answer to the questions of Margaret, told her story. When she came to the mention of her marriage to Leonard Copeland, there was the vindictive exclamation, "Bound to that blood-thirsty traitor! Never! After the way he treated you, no marvel that he fell on my sweet Edmund!"

"Ah! madame, he did not! He tried to save him."

"He! A follower of King Henry! Never!"

"Truly, madame! He had ever loved Lord Edmund. He strove to stay Lord Clifford's hand, and threw himself between, but Clifford dashed him aside, and he bears still the scar where he fell against the parapet of the bridge. Harry Featherstone told me, when he fled from the piteous field, where died my father and brother Robin."

"Your brother, Robin Dacre! I remember him. I would have made him good cheer for your sake, but my mother was ever strict, and rapped our fingers, nay, treated us to the rod, if we ever spake to any of my father's meine. Tell on, Grisell," as her hand found its way under the hood, and stroked the fair hair. "Poor lonely one!"

Her indignation was great when she heard of Copeland's love, and still more of his mission to seize Whitburn, saying, truly enough, that he should have taken both lady and Tower, or given both up, and lending a most unwilling ear to the plea that he had never thought his relations to Grisell binding. She had never loved Lady Heringham, and it was plainly with good cause.

Then followed the rest of the story, and when it appeared that Grisell had been instrumental in saving Copeland, and close inquiries elicited that she had been maintaining him all this while, actually for seven years, all unknown to him, the young Duchess could not contain herself. "Grisell! Grisell of patience indeed. Belle mere, belle mere, do you understand?" and in rapid French she recounted all.

"He is my husband," said Grisell simply, as the two Duchesses showed their wonder and admiration.

"Never did tale or ballad show a more saintly wife," cried Margaret. "And now what would you have me do for you, my most patient of Grisells? Write to my brother the King to restore your lands, and - and I suppose you would have this recreant fellow's given back since you say he has seen the error of following that make-bate Queen. But can you prove him free of Edmund's blood? Aught but that might be forgiven."

"Master Featherstone is gone back to England," said Grisell, "but he can bear witness; but my father's old squire, Cuthbert Ridley, is here, who heard his story when he came to us from Wakefield. Moreover, I have seen the mark on Sir Leonard's brow."

"Let be. I will write to Edward an you will. He has been more prone to Lancaster folk since he was caught by the wiles of Lady Grey; but I would that I could hear what would clear this knight of yours by other testimony than such as your loving heart may frame. But you must come and be one of mine, my own ladies, Grisell, and never go back to your Poticary - Faugh!"

This, however, Grisell would not hear of; and Margaret really reverenced her too much to press her.

However, Ridley was sent for to the Cour des Princes, and returned with a letter to be borne to King Edward, and likewise a mission to find Featherstone, and if possible Red Jock.

"'Tis working for that rogue Copeland," he growled. "I would it were for you, my sweet lady."

"It is working for me! Think so with all your heart, good Cuthbert."

"Well, end as it may, you will at least ken who and what you are, wed or unwed, fish, flesh or good red herring, and cease to live nameless, like the Poticary's serving-woman," concluded Ridley as his parting grumble.

CHAPTER XXX

THE WEDDING CHIMES

Low at times and loud at times,
Changing like a poet's rhymes,
Rang the beautiful wild chimes,
From the belfry in the market
Of the ancient town of Bruges.

LONGFELLOW, The Carillon.

No more was heard of the Duchess for some weeks. Leonard was absent with the Duke, who was engaged in that unhappy affair of Peroune and Liege, the romantic version of which may be read in Quentin Durward, and with which the present tale dares not to meddle, though it seemed to blast the life of Charles the Bold, all unknowing.

The Duchess Margaret was youthful enough to have a strong taste for effect, and it was after a long and vexatious delay that Grisell was suddenly summoned to her presence, to be escorted by Master Groot. There she sat, on her chair of state, with the high tapestried back and the square canopy, and in the throng of gentlemen around her Grisell at a glance recognised Sir Leonard, and likewise Cuthbert Ridley and Harry Featherstone, though of course it was not etiquette to exchange any greetings.

She knelt to kiss the Duchess's hand, and as she did so Margaret raised her, kissing her brow, and saying with a clear full voice, "I greet you, Lady Copeland, Baroness of Whitburn. Here is a letter from my brother, King Edward, calling on the Bishop of Durham, Count Palatine, to put you in possession of thy castle and lands, whoever may gainsay it."

That Leonard started with amazement and made a step forward Grisell was conscious, as she bent again to kiss the hand that gave the letter; but there was more to come, and Margaret continued -

"Also, to you, as to one who has the best right, I give this parchment, sealed and signed by my brother, the King, containing his full and free pardon to the good knight, Sir Leonard Copeland, and his restoration to all his honours and his manors. Take it, Lady of Whitburn. It was you, his true wife, who won it for him. It is you who should give it to him. Stand forth, Sir Leonard."

He did stand forth, faltering a little, as his first impulse had been to kneel to Grisell, then recollecting himself, to fall at the Duchess's feet in thanks.

"To her, to her," said the Duchess; but Grisell, as he turned, spoke, trying to clear her voice from a rising sob.

"Sir Leonard, wait, I pray. Her Highness hath not spoken all. I am well advised that the wedlock into which you were forced against your will was of no avail to bind us , as you in mind and will were contracted to the Lady Eleanor Audley."

Leonard opened his lips, but she waved him to silence. "True, I know that she was likewise constrained to wed; but she is a widow, and free to choose for herself. Therefore, either by the bishop, or it may be through our Holy Father the Pope, by mutual consent, shall the marriage at Whitburn be annulled and declared void, and I pray you to accept seisin thereof, while my lady, her Highness the Duchess Isabel, with the Lady Prioress, will accept me as a Grey Sister."

There was a murmur. Margaret utterly amazed would have sprung forward and exclaimed, but Leonard was beforehand with her.

"Never! never!" he cried, throwing himself on his knees and mastering his wife's hand. "Grisell, Grisell, dost think I could turn to the feather-pated, dull-souled, fickle-hearted thing I know now Eleanor of Audley to be, instead of you?"

There was a murmur of applause, led by the young Duchess herself, but Grisell tried still to withdraw her hand, and say in low broken tones, "Nay, nay; she is fair, I am loathly."

"What is her fair skin to me?" he cried; "to me, who have learnt to know, and love, and trust to you with a very different love from the boy's passion I felt for Eleanor in youth, and the cure whereof was the sight and words of the Lady Heringham! Grisell, Grisell, I was about to lay my very heart at your feet when the Duke's trumpet called me away, ere I guessed, fool that I was, that mine was the hand that left the scar that now I love, but which once I treated with a brute's or a boy's lightness. Oh! pardon me! Still less did I know that it was my own forsaken wife who saved my life, who tended my sickness, nay, as I verily believed, toiled for me and my bread through these long seven years, all in secret. Yea, and won my entire soul and deep devotion or ever I knew that it was to you alone that they were due. Grisell, Grisell," as she could not speak for tears. "Oh forgive! Pardon me! Turn not away to be a Grey Sister. I cannot do without you! Take me! Let me strive throughout my life to merit a little better all that you have done and suffered for one so unworthy!"

Grisell could not speak, but she turned towards him, and regardless of all spectators, she was for the first time clasped in her husband's arms, and the joyful tears of her friends high and low.

What more shall be told of that victory? Shall it be narrated how this wedlock was blest in the chapel, while all the lovely bells of Bruges rang out in rejoicing, how Mynheer Groot and Clemence rejoiced though they lost their guest, how Caxton gave them a choice specimen of his printing, how Ridley doffed his pilgrim's garb and came out as a squire of dames, how the farewells were sorrowfully exchanged with the Duchess, and how the Duke growled that from whichever party he took his stout English he was sure to lose them?

Then there was homage to King Edward paid not very willingly, and a progress northward. At York, Thora, looking worn and haggard, came and entreated forgiveness, declaring that she had little guessed what her talk was doing, and that Ralph made her believe whatever he chose! She had a hard life, treated like a

Charlotte M. Yonge

slave by the burgesses, who despised the fisher maid. Oh that she could go back to serve her dear good lady!

There was a triumph at Whitburn to welcome the lady after the late reign of misrule, and so did the knight and dame govern their estates that for long years the time of 'Grisly Grisell' was remembered as Whitburn's golden age.

Choose from Thousands of 1stWorldLibrary Classics By

Adolphus WilliamWard
Aesop
Agatha Christie
Alexander Aaronsohn
Alexander Kielland
Alexandre Dumas
Alfred Gatty
Alfred Ollivant
Alice Duer Miller
Alice Turner Curtis
Alice Dunbar
Ambrose Bierce
Amelia E. Barr
Andrew Lang
Andrew McFarland Davis
Anna Sewell
Annie Besant
Annie Hamilton Donnell
Annie Payson Call
Anton Chekhov
Arnold Bennett
Arthur Conan Doyle
Arthur Ransome
Atticus
B. M. Bower
Basil King
Bayard Taylor
Ben Macomber
Booth Tarkington
Bram Stoker
C. Collodi
C. E. Orr
C. M. Ingleby
Carolyn Wells
Catherine Parr Traill
Charles A. Eastman
Charles Dickens
Charles Dudley Warner
Charles Farrar Browne
Charles Ives
Charles Kingsley
Charles Lathrop Pack
Charles Whibley
Charles Willing Beale
Charlotte M. Braeme
Charlotte M.Yonge
Clair W. Hayes
Clarence Day Jr.
Clarence E. Mulford

Clemence Housman
Confucius
Cornelis DeWitt Wilcox
Cyril Burleigh
D. H. Lawrence
Daniel Defoe
David Garnett
Don Carlos Janes
Donald Keyhole
Dorothy Kilner
Dougan Clark
E. Nesbit
E.P.Roe
E. Phillips Oppenheim
Edgar Allan Poe
Edgar Rice Burroughs
Edith Wharton
Edward J. O'Biren
John Cournos
Edwin L. Arnold
Eleanor Atkins
Elizabeth Cleghorn
Gaskell
Elizabeth Von Arnim
Ellem Key
Emily Dickinson
Erasmus W. Jones
Ernie Howard Pie
Ethel Turner
Ethel Watts Mumford
Eugenie Foa
Eugene Wood
Evelyn Everett-Green
Everard Cotes
F. J. Cross
Federick Austin Ogg
Ferdinand Ossendowski
Francis Bacon
Francis Darwin
Frances Hodgson Burnett
Frank Gee Patchin
Frank Harris
Frank Jewett Mather
Frank L. Packard
Frederick Trevor Hill
Frederick Winslow Taylor
Friedrich Kerst
Friedrich Nietzsche
Fyodor Dostoyevsky

Gabrielle E. Jackson
Garrett P. Serviss
Gaston Leroux
George Ade
Geroge Bernard Shaw
George Ebers
George Eliot
George MacDonald
George Orwell
George Tucker
George W. Cable
George Wharton James
Gertrude Atherton
Grace E. King
Grant Allen
Guillermo A. Sherwell
Gulielma Zollinger
Gustav Flaubert
H. A. Cody
H. B. Irving
H. G. Wells
H. H. Munro
H. Irving Hancock
H. Rider Haggard
H. W. C. Davis
Hamilton Wright Mabie
Hans Christian Andersen
Harold Avery
Harold McGrath
Harriet Beecher Stowe
Harry Houidini
Helent Hunt Jackson
Helen Nicolay
Hendy David Thoreau
Henrik Ibsen
Henry Adams
Henry Ford
Henry Frost
Henry James
Henry Jones Ford
Henry Seton Merriman
Henry Wadsworth
Longfellow
Henry W Longfellow
Herbert A. Giles
Herbert N. Casson
Herman Hesse
Homer
Honore De Balzac

Horace Walpole
Horatio Alger, Jr.
Howard Pyle
Howard R. Garis
Hugh Lofting
Hugh Walpole
Humphry Ward
Ian Maclaren
Israel Abrahams
J.G.Austin
J. Henri Fabre
J. M. Barrie
J. Macdonald Oxley
J. S. Knowles
J. Storer Clouston
Jack London
Jacob Abbott
James Allen
James Lane Allen
James Andrews
James Baldwin
James DeMille
James Joyce
James Oliver Curwood
James Oppenheim
James Otis
Jane Austen
Jens Peter Jacobsen
Jerome K. Jerome
John Burroughs
John F. Kennedy
John Gay
John Glasworthy
John Habberton
John Joy Bell
John Milton
John Philip Sousa
Jonathan Swift
Joseph Carey
Joseph Conrad
Joseph Jacobs
Julian Hawthrone
Julies Vernes
Justin Huntly McCarthy
Kakuzo Okakura
Kenneth Grahame
Kate Langley Bosher
L. A. Abbot
L. T. Meade
L. Frank Baum
Laura Lee Hope

Laurence Housman
Leo Tolstoy
Leonid Andreyev
Lewis Carroll
Lilian Bell
Lloyd Osbourne
Louis Tracy
Louisa May Alcott
Lucy Fitch Perkins
Lucy Maud Montgomery
Lydia Miller Middleton
Lyndon Orr
M. H. Adams
Margaret E. Sangster
Margaret Vandercook
Maria Edgeworth
Maria Thompson Daviess
Mariano Azuela
Marion Polk Angellotti
Mark Overton
Mark Twain
Mary Austin
Mary Cole
Mary Rowlandson
Mary Wollstonecraft
Shelley
Max Beerbohm
Myra Kelly
Nathaniel Hawthrone
O. F. Walton
Oscar Wilde
Owen Johnson
P.G.Wodehouse
Paul and Mable Thorn
Paul G. Tomlinson
Paul Severing
Peter B. Kyne
Plato
R. Derby Holmes
R. L. Stevenson
Rabindranath Tagore
Rahul Alvares
Ralph Waldo Emmerson
Rene Descartes
Rex E. Beach
Richard Harding Davis
Richard Jefferies
Robert Barr
Robert Frost
Robert Gordon Anderson
Robert L. Drake

Robert Lansing
Robert Michael Ballantyne
Robert W. Chambers
Rosa Nouchette Carey
Ross Kay
Rudyard Kipling
Samuel B. Allison
Samuel Hopkins Adams
Sarah Bernhardt
Selma Lagerlof
Sherwood Anderson
Sigmund Freud
Standish O'Grady
Stanley Weyman
Stella Benson
Stephen Crane
Stewart Edward White
Stijn Streuvels
Swami Abhedananda
Swami Parmananda
T. S. Ackland
The Princess Der Ling
Thomas A. Janvier
Thomas A Kempis
Thomas Anderton
Thomas Bailey Aldrich
Thomas Bulfinch
Thomas De Quincey
Thomas H. Huxley
Thomas Hardy
Thomas More
Thornton W. Burgess
U. S. Grant
Valentine Williams
Victor Appleton
Virginia Woolf
Walter Scott
Washington Irving
Wilbur Lawton
Wilkie Collins
Willa Cather
Willard F. Baker
William Makepeace
Thackeray
William W. Walter
Winston Churchill
Yei Theodora Ozaki
Young E. Allison
Zane Grey